Red Carpet Romeo

(book three of the Royal Romeos series)
by Jenny Gardiner

What people are saying about Jenny Gardiner's books:

"A fun, sassy read! A cross between Erma Bombeck and Candace Bushnell, reading Jenny Gardiner is like sinking your teeth into a chocolate cupcake…you just want more."

--Meg Cabot, NY Times bestselling author of Princess Diaries, Queen of Babble and more, on Sleeping with Ward Cleaver

"With a strong yet delightfully vulnerable voice, food critic Abbie Jennings embarks on a soulful journey where her love for banana cream pie and disdain for ill-fitting Spanx clash in hilarious and heartbreaking ways. As her body balloons and her personal life crumbles, Abbie must face the pain and secret fears she's held inside for far too long. I cheered for her the entire way."

--Beth Hoffman, NY Times bestselling author of *Saving CeeCee Honeycutt* on *Slim to None*

"Jenny Gardiner has done it again--this fun, fast-paced book is a great summer read."

--Sarah Pekkanen, NY Times bestselling author of *The Opposite of Me,* on *Slim to None*

"As Sweet as a song and sharp as a beak, *Bite Me* really soars as a memoir about family--children and husbands, feathers and fur--and our capacity to keep loving though life may occasionally bite."

--Wade Rouse, bestselling author of At Least in the City Someone Would Hear Me Scream

The Lord Chamberlain is commanded by the Queen of Monaforte to invite
Valentina Letizia Beatrice Romeo
To the Marriage of
His Royal Highness, Prince Luca Francesco DeMaio, Duke of Bartolomea
With
Miss Larkin Mallory
At the Cathedral of Santo Giacomo il Maggiore
On Friday, December 20, at 5:00 p.m.

A reply is requested to: State Invitations Secretary, Lord Chamberlain's Office,
Grande Palace of Monaforte,
Porto Castello, Monaforte
Dress: Uniform or white tie attire requested

Ten Years Ago

VALENTINA Romeo had learned early in life that in order to survive, you had to be tough. As the only girl surrounded by six testosterone-laden brothers, she had to be loud to be heard, and—no shrinking violet—you can be sure, she wanted to be heard.

But it wasn't easy, because her brothers were mostly bigger and stronger and liked to put her in her place, which meant Valentina was too often left itching for a fight. How dare those boys tell her she couldn't climb the ancient olive trees with them? And who were they to insist that she couldn't descend into the damp caves on the family estate and go exploring where it was rumored German soldiers hid at the end of World War II? Time and again those boys left her in their dust and feeling bitter that no matter how hard she tried to be one of them, they fought her every inch of the way.

Of course, in their defense, they had some competing interests: regular threats from their parents to take care of their "delicate" sister and protect her not only from outside forces but also from her overly ambitious, tomboyish self meant they were constantly conflicted. They knew if they brought Valentina with them when they went off to pursue their near-daily explorations and investigations on the vast tracts of farmland and the forested hills of *Cantine dei Marchesi Romeo*, on which the Romeo family had been growing and harvesting grapes and olives for six hundred years, they'd be responsible for anything that might go wrong. And what boy in his right mind wanted to carry that burden?

For a respite from that frustrating daily conflict, Valentina looked forward to summertime, when her family joined with their cousins, the royal family from neighboring Monaforte, at a huge seaside compound on the Ligurian Sea in Northern Italy. There the many cousins spent their days on the beach building sand forts and castles—castles being something they were intimately familiar with—and digging for shells and fossils and swimming until they could swim no longer. It was a paradise for children, and while Valentina certainly enjoyed keeping company with her only female cousin, Princess Isabella, it was her older cousin, Prince Luca, who immediately dazzled her.

Luca, who treated her like an equal even though she was six years younger. Luca, who made certain to include his young cousin when the kids hiked up high in the Ligurian hills to capture the view of the sea for miles around them. Luca, who caught a salamander and named it Valentina in his cousin's honor. That was all it took for Valentina to be smitten for life: if she could harbor a crush on a blood relative, well she would have. Instead, she just adored him and cherished the time they got to spend together.

And then Luca showed up the summer of her fourteenth birthday with a new friend—a roommate from university. It was only then that Valentina truly understood how a girl could swoon over a handsome man. Because Parker Hornsby, with his sandy-blond hair, twinkly blue eyes, dimpled cheeks, and brilliant white smile, was indeed swoon-worthy.

"Valentina," Luca said, swooping in to hug his cousin and kiss both her cheeks as was customary and brushing her head of embarrassingly bushy brown hair back off her face. "I missed you so much." He squeezed her nose affectionately. "I want you to meet my friend Parker Hornsby. He's from America. I told him what a magical place *Cieli di Zaffiro* is." Sapphire Skies: it would then become known as the place where she first fell in love.

Valentina took one look at her cousin's new friend and was thunderstruck. Something deep in her gut roiled to life, something she'd yet to recognize, a feeling so powerful it made her scared and happy and nervous and worried, all wrapped up into one untidy heap of swirling emotions that about did her in, they terrified her so.

"Nice to meet you," Parker said, extending his hand to Valentina, which completely threw her off. She'd expected the usual greeting, a kiss on one cheek and then a kiss on the other. So instead of reaching her arm out to shake his hand, she leaned in as if to field his courteous side kisses, and instead his hand jammed into her barely there breasts, and she about died from embarrassment as everyone standing nearby laughed at the mix-up, and so immediately she fled the room, mortified.

When Luca came up to her bedroom to check on her later, her tearstained cheeks thoroughly betrayed her lackluster attempt at feigning indifference.

"Valentina ballerina," he said, scruffing her long dark hair with his fingers.

It was her favorite nickname, one only he used with her. It didn't even make sense because she was so far removed from being a delicate ballerina. He should have called her out for the tomboy she was. Give her a soccer ball and she'd kick pretty much anyone's ass. A pair of ballet slippers? She'd probably slide them on her hands thinking they were mittens.

"Why the long face, my friend?"

Valentina sat on the edge of the bed, swinging her legs and kicking the side of the bed in rhythmic motion, staring out the window, lips pursed, not making eye contact with her cousin.

"What happened that made you run off like you did?" Luca said, pressing her for more details.

Valentina hung her head, so embarrassed. "Nothing."

"Nothing?" He frowned and arched his brow, his bright blue eyes twinkling.

"All right. Fine," she said with a huff. "I thought he was going to kiss my cheeks like everybody always does, and instead he reached out his arm and his hand hit my chest and God, Luca. I mean, really—"

"Oh, sweetie," he said. "Nobody even saw that."

"Of course they did. They all laughed."

"They just laughed at the confusion of the thing. No one was laughing at you, and no one noticed if his hand even touched you."

She crossed her arms over said chest, about which she'd become acutely self-conscious what with all the other girls her age having blossomed into B-cup babes by then while Valentina was still about as flat as the field of sunflowers her parents had planted for her brother Matteo near their manor home. The last thing she wanted was anyone making cracks about that virtual concavity resting atop her chest.

"Hey." He leaned forward and coaxed her chin with

his finger so she was facing him. "It's okay, Valentina. Believe me, we all adore you to the moon and back."

She frowned. "It's just that, well, Luca, I'm a teenager, and look at me." She swept her hands along her T-shirt-clad chest, which was sporting a bra out of pure youthful desire, certainly not need. The giant pouf of out-of-control hair didn't help matters, nor did the splotches of acne plaguing her face.

Her cousin reached around and wrapped her in a bear hug. "Oh, now. Trust me, you are perfect just the way you are. And believe me, before you know it, this is going to be the least of your problems. Pretty soon we'll be beating the boys away. They're going to be pounding down the doors just to get to you. Don't you worry your pretty little head anymore, okay? Besides, you'll always be my Valentina ballerina."

It took Valentina a few days, but eventually she started actually speaking to Parker Hornsby, and that swirling mess of confusing feelings soon crystallized into what was irrefutable in her young mind: love. She was indeed convinced she was in love with Luca's good friend, who was handsome and athletic, and oh, the timbre of his voice was like hearing the very church bells she'd imagined would peal on their wedding day.

Besides, he always picked her for his side when they played pickup soccer on the beach, so she knew the feelings were mutual. But as the summer days progressed, she yearned desperately to somehow advance beyond the stage of goal assists and into something more intimate, like a first kiss. She even practiced her nascent kissing skills for the day they would come in handy, pressing into service a stuffed monkey she slept with. She had no idea how she would drum up the nerve to act, but she knew she had to; she'd never forgive herself if she let him get away.

One night the cousins built a huge bonfire on the beach. They sat around talking and laughing, the older ones drinking wine and, eventually, some even went swimming. Valentina sat along the shore, her chin to her knees, her arms wrapped tight around her legs, not particularly interested in going into the dark ocean water. Until Parker reached out his hand to her.

"Let's go, short stuff," he said to her, clasping her hand in his as he pulled her toward the water. At first she shook her head, refusing, but, hey, he was holding her hand! How could she say no? She lifted herself off the cold sand and followed him into the surf, laughing and splashing and thoroughly elated because she knew this must be the sign she was waiting for.

She tripped and fell in the shallows, and he leaned forward to help her up. Just as he reached for her, she wrapped her arms around his neck and blurted out those three fateful words—*I love you*—while awkwardly angling her mouth and planting her lips on his as if she were administering mouth-to-mouth resuscitation to a training dummy.

Parker, instead of embracing her, pushed her away.

"Valentina, no!" he said, raking his hand through his hair, clearly put off by her declaration and unwanted advances.

She looked at him with querying eyes, her brow wrinkled, confused at his rejection. "But I thought you liked me."

He shook his head, looking around, which she took to mean he was embarrassed that someone might have seen what transpired. "Of course I like you as my friend's cousin. But you're just a young girl. This"—he pointed back and forth between the two of them—"will never happen, Valentina. I'm a grown-up and you're a child." With that, he turned and raced toward the older boys, leaving her dazed and heartbroken in the cold nighttime tide pool, her eyes filled with tears.

He was right, she thought, stewing over his insensitivity. That would never happen. Because she had too much self-respect to moon over that jerk. But she vowed that day she would no longer be the tomboy buddy to all the guys; she was going to show people like that rotten Parker Hornsby. One day men like him would be swooning over her. *That* she was going to make good and sure of.

Chapter One

VALENTINA Romeo was a hopeless romantic. And nothing screamed romance to her more than a good old-fashioned royal wedding. So when the much-anticipated invitation arrived for the nuptials of her favorite cousin, Prince Luca of Monaforte, she was beside herself with excitement.

The only thing that made her a bit sad was that she would be attending this wedding minus a plus-one since she'd been plunged into a seriously dry spell in the man department for far longer than she cared to admit. It would have been more enjoyable to share in this excitement with someone she loved. Although at least she'd be surrounded by many people *she* loved at this union of their families, and she was stoked. But that wasn't the same as showing up in a gorgeous ball gown with the man of your dreams in white tie beside you, your gloved arm entwined in his tuxedo-clad one. It had been over a year since Valentina had ended a relationship with Roberto Agnese, whose family owned a vineyard not far from Romeo Wines.

The two families had competed on a friendly basis for hundreds of years, and it seemed a good enough fit. Until Valentina finally admitted to herself that she didn't want to spend the rest of her life tied to a man with whom the most she had in common was a bunch of grapes. Of course, Roberto was handsome in that classically Italian way, with wavy, near-black hair and warm brown eyes, but if she were truthful with herself, she'd have to admit he bored her a bit.

Sure, he could be charming, but really all he wanted to do was talk wine. And while wine certainly defined Valentina's life in many ways, she knew there was far more to living than just that. Besides, she needed a man to challenge her, someone to keep her on her toes, keep her guessing a bit, maybe make her work at the relationship. Not that she was looking for a beast of burden for a boyfriend, but at the end of the day, Valentina felt a bit *meh* about Roberto. So while it left a bit of a vacancy in her life, she knew it was wrong to keep leading the poor guy on, and she was comfortable with the decision. Just maybe a little lonely. And perhaps a little hot and bothered, because well, it had been a year.

For much of that year she'd been plenty busy with decorating and putting the many finishing touches on the new Marchesi Romeo Wines headquarters, a state-of-the-art, earth-friendly, mammoth structure built into a hillside on the Romeo estate, designed to integrate technology and nature seamlessly. Valentina oversaw the hiring and management of a team of top decorators and devoted all her efforts into ensuring the outcome she desired. The building had met with resounding approval both in the architectural world and the wine world and had become a tourist destination while serving as Romeo corporate office headquarters.

But many months had passed since she'd wrapped that up, and now that she wasn't consumed with that project, she felt a bit rudderless: no man, no compelling work, and no fun made Valentina a dull girl. If not dull, then at least bored. And to make matters worse, try as she might to come up with someone—anyone—to escort her to this wedding, she couldn't think of a man. Which made her feel like either a bit of a loser or perhaps even a man-snob: either no guy was interested in her or she couldn't deign herself to be interested in any guy. Either way, well, it didn't bode well for her.

Maybe the timing of Luca's wedding couldn't be better: a change of scenery and a Christmastime wedding in one of her favorite places, the magical country of Monaforte. Add to that a wonderful reunion of family and friends, some seasonal snowfall and holiday cheer, with lots of parties and gorgeous clothes to wear and of course champagne, which she adored, and it seemed this wedding was just what the doctor ordered. It sounded perfect. And if she didn't have a date for the wedding of the year, well, she could always force her brothers to dance with her. Throw in all her male cousins, and that should keep her occupied for a good part of the reception.

Now all she needed was the perfect wardrobe for the occasion, which would be easy peasy with her fashion model/soon-to-be-sister-in-law Taylor McFarland as her shopping companion.

Taylor had just finished the fall fashion week circuit and had returned to *Cantine Marchesi Romeo*, the estate of the

Romeo family, headed by her fiancé Alessandro. Valentina barely gave her time to rest her feet before she rallied her to the cause.

"Come along," she said, pulling at Taylor's hand as Sandro tried to hold her down with his. "Time's a-wasting, lady. We've got to get ready for this big *festa*. If I have to attend a wedding alone, then I am determined to at least be the envy of everyone at this shindig."

Taylor lifted her brow. "Um, isn't that the role of the bride?"

"Okay, fine. I'll give her most of the attention. But I want some of it flowing my way. I don't want to be the sad-sack spinster at this thing."

Taylor looked at her and motioned from her head to her feet with her arm. "I'm pretty sure no one is going to view you as the sad-sack spinster." She crossed her arms, resting her chin on her hand. "Between those smoldering brown eyes of yours, that enviable long, brown hair with those soft curls women would pay good money to own, and let's not even talk about your gorgeous figure—"

"Ugh, please," Sandro said. "Would you not talk about my sister's attributes in mixed company? I really do not want to be privy to that. She is my sister, after all."

Taylor playfully slapped his arm. "Oh Sandro, stop. She's a beautiful young woman. You should be proud of who she's grown up to be."

"Of course I'm proud of who Valentina is," he said. "I just don't want to hear about all the physical traits that are going to lure some stupid guy to her like she's baiting a mousetrap or something. Oh, and this guy is never going to be good enough for her, by the way. Which means it will be up to me to set him straight and send him packing."

"You sound like a caveman with that primitive talk," Taylor said with a growl as her fiancé pulled her into his arms and planted a long, passionate kiss on her lips.

"As we were saying about icky things siblings don't want to witness." Valentina tapped her foot and looked at her watch, her impatience growing by the minute. "*Andiamo*, Taylor. Let's go, already!"

She pulled Taylor by the shoulders and couldn't believe her ears when Taylor and Sandro's mouths popped as the kiss broke from her disengaging them. "Ewwwww. Just for that, Sandro, you owe me a gown for this wedding. I'll have to use my money for therapy to get over this mortifying episode."

Alessandro shook his head but pulled out his wallet, handing Taylor his credit card. "You two will be the most beautiful women in attendance, my treat. Now go, before I lock Taylor in my room for the next week."

"We need to get out of here, Taylor," Valentina said as she pretended to stick her finger down her throat and gag. "Any more of this saccharine overdose from my brother and I'll end up in a sugar coma. Love you, brother dearest! Thanks for the wardrobe boost. Ciao, ciao!"

Chapter Two

PARKER Hornsby double-checked his packing list once more with his sister Gisele.

"Okay, so white tie, white shirt, white vest, white gloves," he said, enumerating each item he needed to be sure was laid out for the upcoming trip to Monaforte for his good friend Luca's wedding.

"Check," she said as she held each item aloft and inspected it as if it were an alien creature. It wasn't often one was required to don white tie, and the accoutrements of the style hearkened back to a time long forgotten, when lords and ladies of the manor decked out in formal wear for dinner each night and butlers and ladies-in-waiting catered to their every need.

"Black patent leather dress shoes, braces, cufflinks, tailcoat, tuxedo trousers, formal black overcoat." He lifted his coat by the hanger, looked closely at what he thought was a stain, then brushed off what turned out to be a piece of lint.

"Parker, you are going to look dashing at this white tie wedding," Gisele said. "Amanda Covington will rue the day she dumped you for that weasel."

"'That weasel' happens to be my investment partner." He ran his fingers through his blond hair. "And I can't afford to risk that relationship right now—"

"So you just let go of the girlfriend—even though I'm glad you did, mind you—and not even try to exact revenge?" Gisele pulled a ponytail holder from her wrist and secured her long, wavy blond hair into a loose side-braid.

"It obviously wasn't much of a relationship if she jumped ship that easily," Parker said. "Better to have learned that before things got too serious. Besides, it's been months since I found out about the two of them sneaking around behind my back. I'm totally over it."

"Well, you're a better man than I. I'd cut that beyotch off at the knees if I were you."

"Probably just as well you're not me then. Or a man, for that matter. You always were the emotional one in the family." He winked, his blue eyes twinkling.

"The good news is that her loss is my gain since now I get to come as your date!" She jumped up and down like a giddy schoolgirl. "And I get to wear a ball gown, and oh my God, do I have to curtsy before the queen?"

He shook his head. "You're not a royal subject of Monaforte, so no, you do not have to curtsy—or bow, for that matter—before the sovereign."

"So what do I do when I meet her?"

"Same thing you did the first time you met Luca," he said. "You smile, say 'pleased to meet you, Your Majesty'—although with Luca, it was 'Your Highness'—and then move on. After all, there will be a few hundred people in line behind you to greet her as well, so I'd suggest you avoid sharing your life story with her."

Gisele grabbed a pillow from the bed and thwacked her brother on the head with it. Then she turned to face the mirror that was hanging over the dresser in his room. "*Your Majesty*," she said, clasping her hands together, bowing her head and curtsying anyhow. "I'm going to be in the presence of majesty!"

Parker aimed his finger at his temple and twirled it in a circular motion. "You're a crazy lady, you know that?" He cast his broad, white smile at her, that smile that every woman—even little sisters—found irresistible.

"Crazy about going to a real live palace and meeting an actual queen. Hell yeah, I am!" she said. "Now, if we've got you all sorted out, I need to return to my own packing, because I don't want to forget a thing."

"Have at it, sis. Driver will be here for us at six."

"Ooooh, good," she said. "And maybe on the plane ride over you can grill me on royal protocol and Monaforte's history. I don't want to mess anything up. And I can't help but think how charming it all is, just your plain old American girl marrying a prince."

"Hate to break it to you, but I'll be sound asleep on this flight, and if you know what's good for you, you will be too. We've got a packed scheduled once we get to Porto Castello. A driver will be waiting at the airport to pick us up and take us to the palace."

"Where we'll actually sleep! In a palace. Under thirty-thousand-thread-count sheets!"

"I'm pretty sure they don't make sheets with that high of a thread count," he said. "Just please, play it cool and do you best to not act like a starstruck teenager. I've got my reputation to uphold, you know."

She rolled her eyes. "Please, Parker. All you ever think about is your image and your reputation. I think you're the only boy in your high school who never did anything wrong just so it wouldn't haunt you into adulthood."

"That's right. I've got a strong moral compass, and you are going to be sure no one thinks I'm the exception to the rule in our family." He smiled and swatted her on the behind. "Be ready to take the elevator down at five minutes to six."

"Play it cool, play it cool, play it cool," Gisele muttered out loud as she stared at the cream-colored Rolls-Royce Phantom that was going to be their ride from the airport.

"You're saying that out loud," Parker said through closed lips. "Remember the part about playing it cool? That means you don't tell everyone you're trying to do so. You just do it."

While he was glad to have been able to bring his beloved sister along for this exciting event, he really didn't want to have Luca's family thinking they'd invited someone who'd just fallen off the turnip truck.

"Fine," she said with a disappointed grumble. "But I mean seriously, Park, look at this ride. I feel like we should be in a parade or something, take advantage of the situation. I could just stick my hand out the window and wave like the queen probably does, and they wouldn't even know it wasn't her! I could be impersonating royalty, and it would be our secret."

"Gisele, I am so glad you're getting all your awkward gawkiness out of the way before we meet up with Luca's family. It was a good strategy to do it that way, so thanks." He knew damned well that wasn't her game plan—she didn't even have one—but he figured maybe she'd now take the hint and make it that. He could always hope.

Parker reached into his pocket and took out his phone, pulling up a text from Luca. "After you meet Jerome at baggage claim, let me know so I can be sure I'm back to the palace for your arrival," he read aloud.

Jerome had indeed met them, in full royal-driver regalia: black cap, leather gloves, black topcoat. He greeted Parker with a warm hug; they'd gotten to know one another over the years when Parker had visited Luca in Monaforte, so it was a reunion of sorts. Parker was so looking forward to this whole gathering as a happy reunion: he needed a little injection of joy in his life.

While professionally life had certainly agreed with him over the past few years, and he was now making more money than he could ever know what to do with, personally things weren't so great. First there was the whole Amanda thing, what with him finding her and his business partner William practically dry-humping in a dark corner of a bar while at an investor conference when they thought he'd gone off to bed.

It's not that he really missed Amanda much; she'd been fine enough to date, but he was never going to get serious with her. She was more like someone to attend events with and scratch that sexual itch for a while. But when it got down to it, while beautiful, she was really sort of boring, and he found himself always having to work too hard make conversation. It had become such an effort, and he wanted a relationship to be much less labor-intensive. And interesting. And fun. And maybe even challenging, but not challenging in having to figure out what to say to a partner.

The biggest victim in the fallout was his ability to trust—a double whammy considering it was both his girlfriend and his business partner who'd knocked that down. He had no preconceived notions about the world being fair or even honest, but he held out hope for both, so when he was proven wrong on both counts, it sort of left him in a gray funk. Which meant he hadn't bothered to start dating again—quite frankly, he was certain it would be a while until someone intrigued him enough to even consider trusting her. And because of all that, he was feeling pretty glum.

So a Christmastime wedding in wintry Monaforte was just the thing he needed to de-gloom a bit and get into the spirit of things. Maybe throw in a diversionary skiing holiday in the Alps, and he was going to be a happy man.

Jerome opened the back door of the Rolls and motioned for Gisele to have a seat, then nodded to Parker to do so as well.

"Parker. I'm sorry, I'll shut up just as soon as Jeeves gets in the car, but oh my God, look at this thing!" She caressed the leather upholstery, which was nearly as soft as a baby's bottom. She moaned and Parker threw her the stink-eye. "I assume this means I can't take my shoes off and bury my toes in the plush carpet?" She smiled broadly and elbowed him in the ribs.

"Save it for when you're in your room at the palace. There you can gawk and behave like a tourist all you want. But in public now, you're officially cool as a cucumber."

Parker had enjoyed this ride from the airport many times but had never done so at Christmastime. So it was almost like new for him too, watching the hills cloaked in a blanket of snow that Jerome told them had fallen overnight.

"Weather gets unpredictable at this time of year," Jerome said. "I remember a few years back we had two feet of snow by Christmas Day."

"Let's hope we don't get that much or I'll be stuck here for the holidays rather than being on my ski holiday."

"There could be worse places to be snowed in, mind you," Jerome said.

"Understatement of the ye-ar," Gisele said in a singsong voice as her brother rolled his eyes at her.

"Play it cool, remember?" he mouthed to her.

"Look up on that hill." She pointed to a stone cottage decorated with pine roping and wreaths, wisps of gray smoke curling from the chimney. "That enchanting cottage. It's like right off of a postcard."

"Or like out of Hansel and Gretel," her brother said. "Maybe the smoke is coming from the kid-sized oven inside." He gave her a wink and tickled her stomach.

"Stop. That's so gross. Don't ruin my fantasy coming to life right before my very eyes."

On the narrow two-lane road, they passed rolling white hills peppered with spotted black-and-white cows. Stacked-stone fencing that delineated property lines was seasonally decorated with huge red bows. Houses, aglow for the holidays, were festooned with white fairy lights that were visible even in daytime. Parker had to admit it really did feel magical. He'd always loved Monaforte—in some ways it felt like he was returning home at this point, he'd been here so many times. With his parents now both gone, the only thing keeping him home anymore was Gisele, and with her joining him, it was a special treat to celebrate the holidays where it felt most festive.

Soon the countryside yielded to city as farmland gave way to large Gothic-style buildings. The architecture of Monaforte reflected the ebb and flow of history throughout Europe with the mixture of building styles seamlessly forming a cohesive sense of culture and grandeur. Parker could feel his shoulders loosen up and his breathing slowing down as the luxury car made its way down the road to town. He glanced over at his sister who looked as if she was desperate to not explode while keeping a secret of utmost importance.

"You okay, sis?"

She side-eyed him. "Only desperate to squeal in excitement is all," she said, pointing out the window at a huge building with tall spires and gargoyles.

"That, my sweet little sister, is where you'll be staying in Monaforte."

Her eyes grew wide. "You are so full of it. I mean seriously, that's like some massive museum or government building or something. Parliament maybe."

He shook his head. "Nope. It's the Grande Palace of Monaforte. AKA home sweet home for you for the next week or so."

She let out a loud, low whistle. "Ho-ly crap. That is going to be so much fun to explore."

"Gisele, you can't just run roughshod over the place. It's their home. Not to mention a national treasure and historic landmark and all sorts of other things. It's filled with palace guards, and trust me, you go where they tell you to go, but no sneaking off on some sort of expedition."

She thrust out her lower lip. "Fine, you spoilsport. But

if they invite me…"

The Rolls passed through the palace gates, the gold-leafed dueling-griffin crest festooning each of the parting gates, then came to a stop on the pebbled driveway just to the side of the grand marble staircase. Awaiting their arrival were Luca and his bride-to-be, Larkin Mallory, the petite blonde he'd met during Fashion Week in Milan.

They both ran to their friends. "It's about bloody time, mate." Luca greeted his good friend with a bear hug. "You remember Larkin?"

"Of course, how could I ever forget?" Parker reached for her and kissed both of her cheeks. A funny Monafortian tradition for two Americans to do, but it made sense since she was becoming part of the royal family. "Of course, Luca, you know Gisele, but Larkin, I'd like you to meet my impish little sister, Gisele, whom we will all have to keep an eye on because I have a sneaking suspicion she is going to deliberately get lost in the hallowed halls of the palace so she never has to return to the States."

They all laughed.

"Oh, you all think that's so funny, but seriously. I wouldn't even miss my job. And you'd never even notice me here." She swept her arm across the front of the palace, indicating the breadth of the place.

"Well, size does matter," Luca said, laughing.

Larkin rolled her eyes. "Let's leave the boys to their bad jokes, and we'll get you settled in. Welcome to Monaforte, where anything is possible!"

Parker hoped she was right, and maybe this wedding would be just what the doctor ordered to pick up his spirits.

Chapter Three

VALENTINA always loved taking the train from Tuscany to Monaforte—the tracks wound through her beloved Chianti countryside, the hills now dressed for the holidays in a festive dusting of snow, past the brilliantly white Carrara marble mines, then high into the Appenines, now deep with snow. After she changed trains in Milan, the next train worked its way into the snow-capped Alps. The scenery on this trip changed so dramatically with the seasons, it was with great anticipation she looked forward to seeing how it differed from the summertime when high mountain pastures were dotted with cows, their bells clanging in the summer winds like Mother Nature's concerto. Now the cows were tucked safely in barns at lower altitudes to wait out the harsh winter months, and recreational skiers laid claim to the steep mountain slopes.

As the train approached Porto Castello, Valentina became antsy with wanting to finally be there, she so loved Monaforte. There was something about this magical country that made her heart sing. The train chugged along countryside peppered with stone farmhouses, the warm glow of tungsten lights in the houses set against the twilight sky making her want to cozy up inside them by the fire with a mug of hot cocoa and a good book. Wisps of smoke curled from the chimneys, and homes twinkled with strands of fairy lights that framed them in honor of the Christmas season.

The glow of the city grew nearer, and with it, the towering Gothic buildings with their intricate architectural flourishes and pointed arches and flying buttresses. Statues abounded, many of ancient Greek and Roman gods and mythical figures, but others of monarchs of Monaforte past.

Soon the familiar palace came into view: the massive stone structure capped with crenellated battlements, turrets, and spires, replete with stone gargoyles frozen as sentinels atop the castle. It was the stuff of fairy tales, and a place where Valentina had spent much time while growing up. The tall wrought iron fence embellished in gold flourishes and capped with gold fleurs-de-lis surrounded the palace and was aglow with white fairy lights and wrapped in pine roping, the main gates adorned with large wreaths. Banners announcing the upcoming nuptials were suspended from streetlamps.

The train rolled into the exquisite Belle Époque-style station, its row of monumental arches with doorways opening to the interior just as the sun was setting. Between each arch were marble sculptures, and hovering above was a wide band of windows. A massive clock tower hovered rose above it all. When the train came to a stop, Valentina grabbed her large suitcase and garment bag with the many dresses she'd brought for the next week's worth of celebrations and clambered down the steps into the station, which was bustling with activity. It smelled of fresh pine and mulled wine, and she wanted to just stop to take in the excitement of the season.

Next to Florence, Porto Castello was one of Valentina's favorite European cities, with its blending of city and seaside and spectacular mountain views in the distance. It was a city that felt both deeply historic yet always ready to reinvent itself with the times. But steeped most in the tradition was the royal family—her cousins—the Eastons of Monaforte. It had been ages since she'd seen any of them; their summers spent holidaying at the seaside compound in Northern Italy had long since passed, and now that all the cousins were grown, their lives had taken on more responsibility and hence allowed for less free time for gathering. This wedding would be a wonderful chance to reconnect.

Valentina made her way through the terminal and out the main entrance, down the wide steps to where she saw Jerome awaiting her.

"Jerome!" she said as she raced down the steps. "It's been too long!"

He smiled. "Miss Valentina, so lovely to have you back."

"I hear you've been a busy man."

He blushed. "Another one on the way, in fact."

She patted his back. "So happy for you. And I hope someday you'll have a good night's sleep again."

He smiled, handing Valentina an envelope. "Orders to deliver upon your arrival, a schedule for the week for all those who are wedding attendants."

She clapped her hands with excitement. "It's not every day you get to be in a royal wedding. Even if it is for my cousin who hardly seems royal to me anyway."

He nodded. "It is going to be quite a memorable event. I know Luca would be devastated if you weren't a part of it."

He ushered her into the car for the short ride to the palace, and before she knew it, the palace gates were looming.

"I dunno," she said. "There is just something about Monaforte. I can't put my finger on it. But magic happens here. I love this place."

He winked at her. "It is a place of wonder. And even more perfect with you here."

Once through the palace gates, he parked and helped her out of the car.

"I feel like I'm home again."

Lady Sarah, lady-in-waiting to Queen Ariana, greeted Valentina as she entered the Grande Foyer, which was filled with works of art from the Middle Ages through the Renaissance, priceless paintings and sculptures and tapestries that would have otherwise found their way to museums were they not the treasures of the family.

Valentina was used to opulence. After all, her family's palazzo was the stuff of royalty from the days when Italy was divided into various principalities, all run by royal entities. Her ancestors were powerful men—because of course back then it was the men who ruled with an iron fist—who held sway over the people, and while most often they were benevolent leaders, nevertheless, they benefited from the power and wealth with vast tracts of property and a number of palazzos that belonged exclusively to the Romeo family.

Of course there was the main home, but they also owned swaths of land in other regions of Tuscany. But nothing, despite the grandeur of her own home, could compare to the Grande Palace of Monaforte. Especially because somehow this massive structure of architectural genius also managed to convey a feeling of home. Though perhaps that was because she'd spent so much time visiting during her childhood, so the place was overrun with memories of holidays and family events, the kids running roughshod throughout the place. And now she was back for Luca's wedding. It was hard to believe they were all grown-up enough for this!

"Darling, it's been ages," Sarah said, enveloping Valentina in a hug.

"Auntie Sarah, so wonderful to see you!" She referred to Sarah as an aunt, even though in reality it was Ariana who was her aunt. But Sarah served as the queen's surrogate because, well, the queen was a busy woman. And Sarah was a perfect substitute for Ariana as she shared her calm demeanor and could anticipate the queen's intents long before she even expressed them.

"Your cousin has planned a busy several days, so you best make sure you are well rested for things. That said, there's a reception that begins in an hour, and Luca has requested your presence. All the wedding attendants will be there so you can all meet and become friendly."

Valentina's family would arrive later in the week; she was needed here by this evening to participate in the pre-wedding events that would involve the attendants, so for now she would be on her own. Which was fine by her.

"Perfect," she said. "If I can have an hour to refresh myself, I'll be totally ready to go."

"Wonderful." Sarah motioned for a footman to retrieve Valentina's luggage. "Let me get you situated and maybe you'll even have a chance to close your eyes."

Valentina lifted a brow. "Are you kidding?" She pointed at her face. "It takes ages to achieve this look. Roma wasn't built in a day, after all." She giggled. This was going to be such a wonderful week. She couldn't wait for the festivities to begin.

Chapter Four

PARKER flattened his hands down his suit jacket and turned sideways to assess himself in the mirror. "How do I look?" he asked his sister.

Gisele reached for a blue can from the bathroom counter, shook it hard, then squirted some foam into her hand. After spreading it over her palms, she started working it through Parker's blond hair as he tried to bat her hands away.

"What are you trying to do to me?"

"Relax," she said, running her fingers through his hair, positioning the strands just so. She held up the can to read the label. "It's called salt-infused surf foam spray blow-dry."

He rolled his eyes as he grabbed the can from her, inspecting the label. "So am I supposed to eat this or wear it? Or surf while eating and wearing it? And were they trying to fit as many adjectives as possible into the name of that product?"

She pressed her hands to his lapel and gave his tie a final tug to tighten it. "Be glad I didn't use the Cityswept finish spray—I think it's almost like applying real pollution-particulate grit to your hair!" She laughed. "Besides, don't be uptight! You just seemed a little too buttoned-up. I wanted to make you look a bit more chill. Relaxed. The way you used to be, before you got your knickers in a wad after Amanda. By the way, you look handsome as always, brother dearest. If I wasn't your sister, I'd do you."

He shook his head. "I know you say that for shock effect, but it's probably best if you keep those comments to yourself over the next week. Somehow I don't think the queen will quite understand the translational humor in that."

She shook her head. "Lighten up, Park. You know I'm just trying to get you in the right frame of mind for this weekend. I want you to have fun. And maybe actually find some gorgeous young woman who *will* do you. Because honestly, you've been sort of a pain in the ass since that whole Amanda debacle. I mean, I know she wasn't 'the one' and stuff, but still, she didn't do you any favors. When someone cheats on you, it just can't do wonders for your self-esteem, and I feel like you've been in a trough since then. So tonight I'll be your cheer squad with my pretend megaphone, saying 'go team go.'" She pounded her fists in the air, rah-rah style.

"Thanks, G." He gave her a quick peck on the cheek. "Not sure I'm ready to take that plunge again though." He splashed on some cologne, then took a quick slug of his bottled water.

"So then don't plunge." She waved her hand in dismissal. "You aren't obligated to marry anyone. Just sleep with them."

He spewed his water on that comment. "Honestly, I don't know where your bold frankness comes from."

She shook her head. "How quickly we forget. Mom was just as brazen as I am. And you loved that about her.

I'm just trying to keep the torch alive. Now go, my favorite brother. Go forth and multiply."

"Um, first, I'm your only brother." He lifted one finger then another as he enumerated his thoughts. "And second, trust me, you do not want me multiplying."

"Au contraire," she said. "I cannot wait to be an auntie to your sweet little babies."

His eyes grew wide. "You're scaring me, G. The last thing on my mind is babies."

"Okay, fine," she said. "But how about at least get your mind back to the practice that leads to babies. I'd be happy if you would just go back there again. Not that I'm actually concerned about your sex life, but I am worried about your overall well-being, and it seems that with the end of that dingdong Amanda came the entrance of the somber-sided Parker who stopped being cheerful and having a good time. And lest we forget, all work and no play makes my brother a very cranky boy. So go find yourself some gorgeous princessy type to bang. And have fun!"

He shook his head, pinching the bridge of his nose. "I'll totally pretend you didn't just say that," he said as he stuck the apartment key in his pocket. "In the meantime, sorry you can't join me tonight, but it seems it's just the wedding attendants, so you're on your own for the evening. Your dinner is going to be delivered shortly, and there's plenty available on Netflix to keep you busy for the night."

She walked around her brother, her hands behind her back, setting one foot slowly in front of the other, feigning innocence. "I suppose this means it's not okay for me to go exploring the palace on my own then?"

"Suffice it to say I will banish you to the dungeon if I

learn you have done anything other than stay right here in our lovely, comfortably appointed, and spacious palace guest apartment, got it?"

She wrinkled her brow. "Okay, fine. But I can only be a prisoner in the tower for so long."

He tapped her nose. "Remind me again why you didn't pursue a career in acting? You'd have made a great drama queen."

"My second act is sure to follow. In the meantime, ta-ta!" she said, blowing kisses as Parker opened the door to leave. "I expect to not see you here the rest of the night. Because that'll mean you've found someone to cozy up to. Good night!" She waved her hands as he walked out the doorway.

Once the door closed behind him, he leaned back, pressing himself against the outside of it, knowing as he did that his irrepressible sister might well find herself getting into all sorts of mischief in this massive land of hide-and-seek where they were guests for the next week.

The reception was just getting underway when Parker arrived in the Blue Ballroom, one of the smaller public spaces in the palace, although small was relative since even this room could comfortably hold more than a hundred guests. The dramatic space—with windows hung with heavy, plush, royal-blue velvet draperies corded in gold—was aglow with candles. Matching gilt-trimmed blue velvet settees were arranged throughout the room to allow for intimate mingling amongst guests.

Mahogany floors gleamed with a high-polish finish, and the coordinating paneled walls with carved friezes lent the room an almost clubby feel in its opulence. A long table stood in the middle of the room, formally set with candelabras, crystal goblets, and crystal wineglasses, along with official palace china. This event was intended to include just the bride, groom, and their twenty attendants. Luca had told Parker that not even the queen or Prince Enrico would be in attendance; he and Larkin wanted this to be a comfortable evening in which all their friends were able to relax and enjoy each other's company without the formality attendant in most royal events.

In the far corner stood a twenty-foot-tall pine Christmas tree and, on the tips of the branches, actual candles burned. Parker couldn't help but think that back home in the States the fire marshal would stand guard with a hose at the ready. It was sort of charming that here in Monaforte they took it on good faith that a Christmas tree wouldn't ignite into a conflagration. Something about Monaforte was all about trusting that things would be okay. He liked that about the place. In his business he spent his life working with contracts and agreements and signing paperwork till his fingers practically bled. In triplicate. There was little that happened on a handshake and with basic trust in the end result. Everything was about ensuring a nonlitigious outcomes. Sometimes that became tiresome. There was such charm to this Old World way of life.

"Parker," he heard a voice say to him as he turned around. It was Luca, who was standing hand in hand with Larkin.

"Ahhh, the two lovebirds," Parker said, greeting them both with the customary two-cheek kiss he'd grown used to during his visits here. "Hard to believe this day has arrived already. I'm so honored to be a part of your marriage celebration. And Larkin, darling, you look positively sumptuous."

"You flatter me too much." She fluttered her eyelashes in pretend flirtation. "Believe me, Parker, your absence would have been a glaring presence. We'd miss your beautiful smile and your generous spirit too much if you weren't here, so thank you for making the long trip!"

"I think you know most of the attendants, so please, make yourself at home. But first be sure to get a drink." Luca motioned for him to grab a glass off a passing butler's tray. "I made sure they'd be serving the thirty-year-old scotch you love so much."

"And they wonder why I keep coming back here," Parker said, cocking his eyebrow conspiratorially at Larkin.

"Right?" She winked.

"Of course." Luca grinned. "Wine, women, and the pursuit of happiness."

"The wine and happiness parts sound fine, but as far as the women go, well, I think I'm on a hiatus from them for a while." Parker made a motion with his hands as if pushing away from a table after a too-filling meal.

"A hiatus from women?" Larkin said. "That's unheard of. Certainly not the Parker I've grown to know."

Luca lifted a brow. "Seriously? All this because of that Amanda?" He shook his head. "I don't get it. It's not like you two were really serious or anything."

Parker frowned. "Everyone says that! But it's not a matter of serious or not. It just comes down to trust, and like it or not, she hit me in the solar plexus with that betrayal."

"Fair enough," Luca said. "In that case, it's probably a good thing I stuck you with my cousin for the week then."

"Cousin?"

"Yes. You remember Valentina?"

"Little Valentina? From all those years ago?"

His friend nodded his head. "One and the same. Only not so little anymore. I thought you might get a kick out of seeing her after such a long time."

"Perfect," Parker said. "Maybe we can find a place for a little game of pickup football. She was always the best damned soccer player, what with that left foot of hers."

"You might be surprised at our 'little' Valentina. She's not the teen tomboy you once knew."

"Well, at least I won't have to worry about some predatory woman clinging to me all week long," he said. "It'll be good to have your sweet cousin to talk with. We'll have fun reminiscing."

"Well, speak of the devil," Larkin said. "Here she comes." She pointed to a tall brunette wearing a form-fitting fuchsia sleeveless V-neck sheath, her hair in soft waves to below her shoulders.

Parker took one look at the woman—whose long, slender legs didn't seem to quit—and he about tripped on his tongue. "Where's Valentina?" He looked around. "Is she standing behind that stunning woman in the pink dress? I can't seem to find her."

Larkin shook her head. "The woman in the pink dress *is* Valentina, silly."

Parker's eyes grew wide. *That* was "little" Valentina? The girl who crushed on him that summer back when he was in college? The one he finally had to break it off a bit rudely with so that she would finally stop hanging on him as if he was her boyfriend?

Ch-rist on a stick. "Little" Valentina had certainly gotten past that awkward teenaged stage and then some. His eyes surveyed the woman standing not twenty feet from him. The hot-pink dress fit her stunning figure like a glove: it clung to her magnificent breasts, skirted down her narrow waist, and clutched her near-perfect ass like a hand. Like he suddenly wished his own hand could do.

As she turned so that her back was to him, he could see that her dress had a full-length back zipper that started at the hem and extended to her shoulders. And suddenly all he could think about was how amazing—and easy—it would be to just reach down and slide that zipper all the way up. He could flick that dress off her in two seconds, tops. And then he could get a look at that gorgeous rack of hers teasing him from beneath that fabric.

But ugh. He couldn't think that way. This was Valentina—Luca's little cousin. Luca's little cousin who'd grown into a young woman who was making a hard-on stir to life in his suit pants for the first time in forever. He needed to tamp that down pronto, or this was going to be a long damned night.

Amanda, he thought. *Amanda, Amanda, Amanda.* If ever there was a cock-blocking thought out there, she was it. All he had to do was think back to discovering her in that shadowy corner, her leg wrapped around William's hip, their lower bodies pressed together in a tight grind, the two of them completely unaware of his presence so engrossed were they in the business at hand.

Thank goodness he had that thought to stop him from

focusing on the most beautiful woman he'd laid eyes on in ages. Sadly it seemed he was going to have to invoke his ex's name a lot over the next week, otherwise he'd need to make like a schoolboy and walk around the palace with textbooks covering his crotch every time Valentina was near.

Just as he stared a beat too long at Luca's jaw-dropping cousin, she turned toward him and suddenly their eyes locked for a split second. Recognition dawned in hers just as he pulled his glance away to avoid the inevitable confrontation. Dammit.

And suddenly his getaway escape palace vacation was turning into a long week of likely torment. So much for his sister's wish for him to go get laid. Now he was going to have to fight himself to keep from insisting on it.

Chapter Five

WELL, *shoot.* Somehow in the excitement leading up to the wedding week, Valentina hadn't even considered who else might be an attendant for said nuptials. But crap if it wasn't him standing there, just twenty-some feet away from her, looking even better than she ever remembered him, darn it.

Parker Hornsby. Her nemesis. Or was it frenemy? Because after all, well, before he was dead to her, in a manner of speaking, he was her summer crush all those years ago. Back then they were friends, or at least she'd thought they were. She had even somehow fantasized that they were on their way to something more than just friends. Until he betrayed her by dismissing her outright, like she wasn't good enough for the likes of him.

That hurt her more than he could have ever imagined. But it changed the course of her life in some ways, forcing her to reevaluate who she wanted to be seen as in the eyes of others. And she decided she no longer wanted to be that invisible pipsqueak kid who was always kicking a soccer ball and was practically interchangeable with her many brothers. Nope.

By the time that following autumn rolled around, gone was the girl trying to keep up with a house full of boisterous boys, and in her stead was the new and improved Valentina. She started wearing makeup, even that horrible mascara, which took her weeks to master without leaving a caterpillar trail on her eyelids. She got a cute hairstyle. She became intensely fashion-conscious, devouring issues of *Vogue Italia* the minute they arrived and bravely teetering on high heels as she attempted to don trendy styles. And soon Valentina, the flat-chested tomboy, started to come into her own, blossoming into a stunningly beautiful young woman.

But while she was busy growing up, Parker had clearly been busy filling out, and he'd turned into one fine specimen of manhood, looking too sexy for his own good in what appeared to be a custom-tailored charcoal suit that his strong chest, broad shoulders, and tightly shaped behind filled out just right. His hair was still blond and beach-y looking, and those blue eyes... They were giving poor Valentina flashbacks to her childhood days of mooning over him, yearning for those eyes to stare into her own hazel-brown ones. Darn it, she had to admit: Parker Hornsby was cute when he was in college. But Parker Hornsby, the grown man? Ay yi yi, he was handsome as all get-out.

And now was as good a time as any to show Parker what he missed out on when he shot her down ten years ago. Boy, was she glad she'd worn the hot—emphasis on the word *hot*—pink dress this evening. She knew it made her legs look amazing, and it highlighted her assets just perfectly.

She would let him look all he wanted, but he wasn't going to have the pleasure of anything more than that. No way, no how. She'd sworn him off ten years earlier, and now he could eat his heart out.

"Val," Larkin said, waving her down. "Come here. I understand there's a reunion of sorts in order here."

Valentina strode with confidence in her gray velvet Manolo Blahnik stiletto-heeled vamp-toe pumps toward her cousin and his affianced. She knew she was going to have to dig deep to pull this one off, but she also knew she could handle it.

"Valentina." Luca gestured toward her frenemy. "You remember my old friend from university, Parker Hornsby, right?"

Valentina lifted an eyebrow, feigning curiosity. "Parker," she said slowly as if having to think about it first. "Why, yes... Parker. I remember now—you came down that one summer, didn't you? A long time ago, right?"

Cool as a cucumber.

Parker squinted at her. "Valentina," he said, reaching for her hand, which he pulled up to his mouth and pressed a kiss on the back of. "You've grown into a breathtakingly beautiful woman."

Wait a minute. What? He was complimenting her?

Hmmm... She wasn't prepared for praise. She was hoping maybe he'd be as big a jerk as she tried to remember him being. She pulled her hand away from his lips, placing her flute of champagne in that hand to keep it occupied and away from him. The kiss burned her flesh still, even though his lips were nowhere near her skin anymore.

"Thank you," she said with a noncommittal nod. He could have been asking her the weather forecast, she was that ambivalent. Cool as a cucumber, that was her mantra.

"It's so great to see you two meeting up after all these years," Larkin said. "We thought you'd both enjoy being paired up together for the wedding, so it'll be a really fun week for you both to get reacquainted. In fact, I'm pretty sure—" She glanced at Luca to double-check, nodding her head as he nodded back, then clapped her hands happily. "Yeah, Luca made sure to seat the two of you together at every official function this week."

Valentina's mouth flatlined. "Ah, wow. Great. That's so, uh, thoughtful. But really, you don't have to do that. I'm certain you'd much rather mix and mingle everyone. Wouldn't you?" She knit her brow, trying hard to will them into changing their grand scheme.

"Yeah, well, that is, truly, just so sweet of you guys," Parker said. "But Valentina's right. Surely you'd rather have us spend time with others. Seems the most, well, evenhanded way."

Larkin waved her hand. "Nonsense. You'll have such a great time talking about old times. Besides, it's too late to change things now."

Just then a bell rang, announcing that dinner was about to be served.

"Gotta run," Luca said, grabbing Larkin's hand and steering her toward the center of the table. "We'll talk more later!"

Valentina turned toward her newly minted wedding-week mate. Her face fell. This was going to be the worst week ever.

Chapter Six

"SO," Parker said, taking a deep breath and releasing a sigh that spoke volumes. "Looks like it's you and me against the world then."

Valentina rolled her eyes. "You can say that again." She turned to walk toward the table. "Let's just go get this over with."

He knit his brow. "You make it sound like it's some sort of unpleasant experience."

She threw him a deadpan glare. "Gee, ya think?"

"Sorry if you drew the short straw being 'stuck' with me. I'm sure we can rectify this situation, but I hope you'll at least be able to suffer through the meal with me. I promise I won't bite."

She shook her head. "Look, you made it abundantly clear to me long ago that you wanted nothing to do with me. I'm totally good if you and I just keep it to a minimum, and as soon as we can get this straightened out, we will. But for the time being, it's a dinner. I'm sure I can suck it up and deal with it."

It was Parker's turn to glare. Where'd this chick get her attitude? Suck it up? *Geeze*. "In the meantime, for the benefit of the bride and groom, let's just pretend we're having the time of our lives."

"I'd like nothing better." She pressed her lips together in a forced smile as she reached to pull out her seat, but always the gentleman, Parker beat her to it and grabbed it for her, causing her to nearly tumble over after losing her balance. He reached out and caught her in his arms, leaving them breast to chest, her breath soft on his neck. Her perfume, a citrusy musk combination, smelled downright erotic.

He hardly had a chance to think before she flailed her arms, trying to right herself.

"If you'd just hold on a minute, I'll help you up," he said, shifting to deflect that cursed burgeoning hard-on that was once again trying to make itself known against his will. How could it not, with only a few thin patches of fabric between his chest and her tight nipples? God, this was killing him. He was like a damned pubescent boy all of a sudden.

"I'm perfectly capable of righting myself, thanks." She grabbed hold of the hand of the seatmate to her left side who'd offered an assist, a tall, wavy-haired man Parker suddenly wanted to throttle.

"Okey dokey," Parker said. "I'll just make myself comfortable here, and if you deign me to be worthy of your attention, maybe give me a little tap on the shoulder then?"

She gave him a smirk. "This"—she pointed back and forth between the two of them—"will never happen, Parker. Enjoy your meal."

Touché. In the no-good-deed-goes-unpunished department, clearly Parker's decision not to lead on an impressionable young teenager all those years earlier hadn't been particularly appreciated by said teenager. But surely enough time had passed that she should have gotten over that. While he certainly hadn't been deliberately mean back then, perhaps the forcefulness with which his message was delivered had been received a little harsher than he'd hoped. They were both grown-ups now; he just knew he could reason with her.

He turned to Valentina, who was busy talking with the too-handsome man with smoldering brown eyes who'd helped her up. Parker felt a twinge of jealousy as he watched her laugh and smile and place her hand on the man's forearm while she was making a point. For some inexplicable reason, he suddenly wanted—or was it needed—to be the center of her attention. But how could he do that when she was clearly giving him the cold shoulder?

He thought back to his father, who had charm in spades. Perhaps too much charm since he ended up wooing pretty much any gorgeous woman who wandered into his sphere of influence. His poor mother put up with the man tomcatting around for years before she finally called it quits. But when he wasn't busy betraying her, he was indeed deft with a compliment.

"Would you like a dinner roll?" he said, trying to break the conversational Berlin Wall she'd erected to keep him out.

She threw him an icy glare.

"I'm not sure if I mentioned it yet, but you really have grown into a beautiful young woman," he said, continuing with optimism. What woman could resist a little flattery? His mother had always told him to kill them with kindness. "Of course, it wasn't hard to imagine as you were a pretty girl. Besides, I remember your mother was gorgeous as well." He could not believe he was blathering on with platitudes in the hopes of making headway with a brick wall. More like into a brick wall. He was going to end up with a concussion at the rate he was banging his head.

Finally she turned to face him. "Look, Mr. Hornsby," she said. "While I appreciate your kind remarks, really, there is no need to slather on false blandishments. I know you're just trying to butter me up, and there's no need. What's past is past, and we can just move on and be courteous with each other and then the wedding will be over and we won't have to deal with this any longer. Deal?"

Parker clenched his teeth. *Mr. Hornsby?* Was she kidding him? The good news was Parker loved a good challenge, and the obstinate *Miss Romeo* was going to test his mettle in that regard. Maybe more than he'd like.

Parker scrubbed his fingers through his sea-salt-foam-surfin'-safari-styled hair, wanting nothing more than to sidle up to the nearest butler with a tray full of highball glasses topped off with scotch. That would make him particularly happy right about now. But in the meantime, he was going to have to navigate his way through a meal of lobster thermidor with an ice queen to contend with.

Jenny Gardiner

Sometimes life was so unfair.

Chapter Seven

VALENTINA hoped she wasn't too aggressively chatting up her good-looking seatmate at dinner. She'd already established that he was off-limits; his fiancée was waiting back in their room, so there was no hope with him. Shame as he was awfully easy on the eyes. Then again, so was that miserable rat bastard Parker Hornsby. But for as pleasing as that one might have been to gawk at, maybe even drool over a little, he was impossible on the psyche, and she was not going to ever submit herself to his whims if she had any say in the matter. He'd had his chance with her and he blew it.

Perhaps she wasn't so good at recognizing that a decade was a long time and an age gap can lessen the older you get, and maybe the young version of her with Parker would have been entirely inappropriate, whereas the current version of the two of them would be perfectly socially acceptable—and she dare not think it, but perhaps even desirable.

Shame that her wounded ego refused to entertain that notion. Because he was, well, awfully easy on the eyes. And he had lovely manners. And his voice, that sort of low, soft rumble that reverberated somewhere deep in her belly when he spoke… Well, damn him for that voice. Suffice it to say, she had to continue concentrating on being really furious with him or else she'd find herself succumbing to his charms. Good thing she wasn't that desperate.

Dinner couldn't have ended soon enough though, and as soon as it was clear that the gathering was breaking up for the evening, she excused herself and bade a good night to those at her end of the table, then slipped away from the ballroom.

She'd spent much of her childhood visiting the palace and knew every nook and cranny as if it were her own, so she knew to take a shortcut through the part of the palace with the family apartment. She mounted the red-carpeted steps of the Grande Staircase, followed the Corridor of Elders, stopping to admire portraits of distant relatives on the walls, then turned down a darkened side hallway. She'd reached into her clutch for her phone to turn on the flashlight just as she ran headlong into someone and about jumped out of her skin.

"Ack!" She dropped her phone.

"Eek!" said a female voice attached to a body that quickly bent down to retrieve the phone, handing it to her readily.

"Who the hell are you?" Valentina said, relieved it was a woman. Not that she had anything to fear in the secure palace environment, but still. Dark, spooky halls in castles can unnerve a girl, especially when strangers pop up out of nowhere.

The girl stepped out of the shadows. She was beautiful: medium height and athletic-looking with long, wavy blond hair and soft blue eyes. She looked like she belonged on a beach, not lurking in the shadows of an ancient castle.

"I'm so sorry," she said. "I'm afraid I got a little lost looking for my apartment. I can't quite tell you how I ended up here, but I apologize if I scared you."

Valentina stood back and assessed the stranger. She wore a beige cashmere V-neck sweater with a white T-shirt beneath it, and faded matchstick skinny jeans. She had bunny slippers on her feet.

Valentina started to laugh. "Oh my God," she said, pointing at the girl's feet. "Those."

"I know, right? Only I would get lost in a castle in my bunny slippers. Only thing worse would have been if I was in my pajamas. I hope you can point me toward home before I run into someone important who might have me beheaded for spying or being inappropriately attired for castle-strolling." Her eyes opened wide and she covered her mouth with her hand. "Please tell me I didn't just insult you by suggesting you aren't important."

Valentina shook her head. "Not to worry. I am decidedly not important in the royal pecking order here in Monaforte. By the way, I'm Valentina."

A wash of relief flooded the woman's face. "Thank goodness! I apologize again. I'm Gisele. I just need to find apartment eleven. Have you any clue where it might be?"

"I'm headed that direction myself. I'm number thirteen, so looks like I'm right next door to you. You're here for the wedding?"

Gisele nodded. "Yes. Although I got a little bored tonight, so figured I'd do some exploring. I thought for sure I'd be able to retrace my steps, but maybe I needed to leave a trail of bread crumbs in my wake."

"Good thing there wasn't a wicked witch waiting to toss you in her oven." Valentina winked at her as they followed another narrow hallway. Gisele stared as they passed a suit of armor.

"I'm not worried about that. I've got a mean left hook." Gisele grinned and pretended to slug the armor.

"I like a woman who can fend for herself."

"Any girl with a brother has to do that."

"Tell me about it," Valentina said. "I've got six. I could take any one of them if I had to." She looked upward, rethinking that notion. "Well, I could have when we were all little and they weren't quite so brawny and tall and strong. But still."

"I hear ya. Though I never had to worry about that with my brother. We were always the best of friends."

Valentina smiled. "So sweet," she said. "Those kind make the best husbands, don't they? If they love their sisters, they'll take good care of their partners."

"And yours aren't like that?"

Valentina shook her head. "Oh gosh, of course they are. They all take wonderful care of me. But they are men, and they are Italian, so I guess they can get a little strong-willed and bossy. But my brothers are the best."

"Well, now that we've established we both come from good stock," Gisele said with a nod. "I'm so excited to be here for this wedding. Although with this jet lag, I'm currently more enamored with the idea of finding my room again so I can get to sleep. I hadn't realized quite how exhausted I am."

"This is going to be a fabulous event," Valentina said. "Although I unexpectedly found myself avoiding someone tonight I'd just as soon have never seen again. I'm hoping I can dodge him as much as possible over the next several days."

"Oh, that's a shame," Gisele said. "Sounds unpleasant."

"Just a really annoying person from my past," Valentina said. "No one I'm going to waste another breath worrying about."

"I agree. No sense in bothering with someone like that."

"Say," Valentina said, thinking there was no better distraction from that annoying man than a new friend. "If you'd like, I'd be happy to show you the ropes. I know this place can be a little bit intimidating."

"I'd love that."

"In fact, let's meet for breakfast and I can give you a tour, then maybe we can head into town to do some shopping. The city is lovely at Christmastime."

"Wow, I'm so lucky I got lost when I did and stumbled upon you. This will be so much fun," she said just as they arrived at apartment eleven.

"Meet me at nine in the dining room and we'll go from there."

"Perfect," Gisele said. "And if you need me to fend off that annoying person, like I said, well, I've got a mean left hook."

They both laughed. "Hopefully it won't come to blows, but if it does, I might just call upon your services."

"Worst-case scenario, I'll sic my brother on him."

"So you're here with your brother, then?"

Gisele nodded, inserting her key in the door. "Yes, he's good friends with the groom. His name's Parker. Parker Hornsby."

Chapter Eight

PARKER was just about to send out a search party for his sister when he heard her key turn in the lock.

He turned the knob and opened the door, only to come face-to-face with not just his sister but also none other than the Queen B (and by that he meant Beyotch) of the evening.

"Gisele," he said, his voice stern with anger. "What the hell do you think you were doing out wandering the halls of the palace? I thought I told you not to leave this room."

"This is your brother?" Valentina said, interrupting his reprimand and pointing at his face as if pinning a perp in a line-up.

Gisele nodded. "Yes, and normally he doesn't act like such a jerk in public."

"Au contraire," Valentina said.

Parker glared at her. "The feeling's mutual."

Gisele knit her brow. "Am I missing something here? You two know each other?"

"Unfortunately," Valentina said.

"I have had the pleasure of making Miss Romeo's acquaintance on several occasions," Parker said. "Unfortunately Miss Romeo is known to hold a powerful grudge. Even when there are misunderstandings involved."

"Let's just say your brother is really quite adept at being a total jerk in public and leave it at that."

Gisele frowned. "Um, does this mean we're not getting together in the morning? I mean, I hope you don't judge me based upon my brother's actions, whatever they are. I was really looking forward to our day."

Valentina shook her head as if clearing her thoughts. "Goodness, of course we're still going out tomorrow, Gisele. I wouldn't miss it for the world. After all, as the saying goes, you are not your brother's keeper. I'm totally good forgetting about your connection to him if you are."

Gisele smiled. "Of course I am," she said, clapping. "I can't wait. See you in the morning!"

Parker frowned. What was it with women? Piling on like that. He'd like to think his own flesh and blood would side with him, but even if blood was thicker than water, evidently XY chromosomes trumped blood altogether.

Damn. At the rate things were going, he might just be better off getting on the first plane out of this place.

Once Valentina had left, Parker turned to his sister. "Et tu, Brute?"

Gisele shook her head. "What?"

"Really?" he said. "You sold me out for the chance to spend the day with the likes of her?"

"But she was super nice," she said. "I got lost and she helped me find my way back here. And she offered to be my guide. She's like my palace Sherpa."

He shook his head. "Sherpa?" Honestly, could it get any more ridiculous?

"Yes, she said she could help show me the ropes. You're going to be so busy with all the pre-wedding things, I thought it would be great to do this with someone who knows the place. I mean, how would I know you two hated each other's guts?"

"But once you found that out, maybe you could have thought twice before hurling me under the wheels of the bus, you know. 'Cause right now I sort of feel like a squirrel plastered to the pavement."

She shrugged. "Sorry. I wasn't trying to be mean to you. But I wasn't quite sure what to do, and I figured I don't know her and I do know you and, well, you're my brother and all so you have to forgive me, whereas if I rejected her in favor of you, then she'd never forgive me and there goes my chance for seeing the town with a local."

"She's not even a local!"

"What do you mean?"

"She's Luca's cousin. She's one of the Romeos. I spent a summer at the family beach compound in Italy and got to know her then."

"Please don't tell me you slept with her and left her humiliated in a puddle of tears."

Parker gave her a deadpan look. "You do know it's me you're speaking to?" he said. "Like, I'm not exactly the love 'em and leave 'em type. Besides which, she was a little kid. I was in college. So no, I decidedly did not sleep with her."

"So why does she hate you so much?"

"Because I guess in her childish mind, she'd entertained ideas of something more with me. But like I said, she was a kid and I was an adult. I had to make it clear to her that that was not going to happen. And I guess she then went home and whipped up a voodoo doll with my name on it and has been sticking pins in it ever since. In fact maybe it's her fault Amanda and William betrayed me as they did. It was beyond their control once those pins got jammed into my doppelganger doll."

Gisele pursed her lips. "Huh. Interesting. Very interesting."

Parker looked at the devious look on her face and immediately sensed disaster. "Oh, no you don't," he said. "I know that look. It's that look you get before you decide you're going to meddle in my life. Like the time you signed me up for a Tinder account and failed to tell me. And then you lifted my phone from my pocket and started swiping right on the damned thing to try to get me hooked up with strange women who were at that bar we were both at in midtown."

Gisele laughed. "You must admit, that was pretty ingenious of me."

"Right," he said. "Until those women kept coming up and grabbing my crotch."

"I can't help they were so aggressive! I was just trying to give you a nudge in the right direction."

"You're good at that."

"At what?"

"Being a nudge."

She play-smacked his arm. "I'm not a nudge. I said I was giving you a nudge."

"Nudge, nudge, whatever," he said. "But seriously, you need to be careful with this one. I mean, I'm not going to tell you that you can't hang out with her, but I will ask you to please keep me out of it. I need to be diplomatic here because she's a cousin to Luca and I don't want anything to happen to jeopardize my friendship with him. Deal?"

She sighed. "Much as I'd love to get involved here, I'll play nice and steer clear. But only because I want to go have a fun day in Porto Castello, and doing it with Luca's cousin means, well, she must be royal too, right?"

He rolled his eyes. "Basically the rule of thumb around here is to err on the side of caution. Presume everyone is royal until you know otherwise."

"Oh my God, this is going to be the best week ever."

She gave her brother a huge hug just as he let out an even bigger sigh. Each time he thought the week had bottomed out, the pit grew deeper still. He was going to deserve a medal if he survived this without some major scene that involved the screaming of invectives. At him. By her.

Lord help him.

Chapter Nine

VALENTINA was finishing up her cappuccino when she spied the Jerk escorting his sister down the Grande Staircase on their way to breakfast. She was amused they were taking that route since there were more direct, out-of-the-way paths to get to the dining room without making a huge entrance. Clearly Gisele was enjoying dabbling in the royal experience. And she hadn't seen anything yet; she would no doubt be blown away by the pomp and circumstance of the royal wedding, with guests attired to the hilt in the emblems of royalty. Valentina was going to have fun introducing her new friend to this fantasy world.

She was sort of kicking herself for not realizing sooner that Gisele might belong to Parker. The American accent should have been a dead giveaway. After all, how many Americans would be in attendance at this shindig? Well, actually, plenty, what with the bride being from the States. But still, how many would show up so early before the big event? *Try again, Valentina.* Surely some of Larkin's American guests would come for the pre-festivities. Well, then, how about because Gisele looks so much like the man. Of course she belonged to Parker.

Although it was curious that he'd brought his little sister along rather than a date. Probably because no woman in her right mind would want to be his date anyhow. It would be like going on a date with a gargoyle. Or one of those heavy-breathing dogs with bulging eyes and tongues permanently dangling from the corner of their mouths. Pity the woman who got stuck with him.

Well, never mind that one. Time to put on her game face and tune him out altogether.

"Gisele," she said, her arms open wide as she reached for her new friend, planting cheerful kisses on each cheek. "I trust you slept well last night?"

Gisele rolled her eyes. "Once I was done being lectured by that one," she whispered, aiming her thumb behind her at her brother, who cocked his eyebrow and frowned, evidently able to hear all that she was saying.

Valentina waved her hands dismissively in his direction. "Let's not concern ourselves with that," she said, not even bothering to use a pronoun in reference to the man. "We've got a big day ahead of us. Why don't you grab a croissant from the tray and I'll fix you a quick shot of espresso and we can be on our way."

Gisele leaned in toward Valentina. "I feel sort of bad leaving Parker behind. You sure he's going to be okay?"

"I wouldn't worry about him. He'll find some homeless person to insult or steal a loaf of bread from a starving child. He'll be happy as a clam." She said that loud enough so that he could indeed hear her, and he made a snarly face as if mockingly repeating her words.

"Normally I'd say let's sit and have a relaxed breakfast," Valentina continued. "But, well, the company will be much more palatable once we're away from here. Don't you agree?"

Gisele threw one of those "What can I do? I can't help

it!" looks to her brother and shrugged as Valentina led her out of the dining room and down the hallway toward the awaiting car.

Outside, bright December sunshine reflected off the blanket of snow that covered everything.

"What a perfect day," Gisele said, spreading her arms wide. "I swear I keep pinching myself that I'm actually here. At a palace. For a royal wedding! Which reminds me, what exactly is your connection to the royal family?"

"My family, the Romeos, has been in Italy for hundreds upon hundreds of years. We are from Italian royalty before unification happened in Italy and the royals were shut out. So while technically we are of royal stock, our country no longer recognizes us as such," she said. "The Eastons—the Monaforte royals—are my cousins. My mother, Fabiana, is sister to their father, Prince Enrico. And as such, we spent many hours together as children, and I regard the palace as a second home. Well, that and our family seaside retreat."

Gisele lifted an eyebrow. "Where you met my brother?"

Valentina grumbled. "Unfortunately. Yes. But let's not ruin the day with such talk. I've got lots in store for you."

It had crossed Valentina's mind that perhaps it was insulting for her to diss the woman's brother like that, but honestly, the mere thought of the man made her skin crawl. At least when it didn't make it feel all warm and tingly. All the more reason it was really important to reinforce that he was the Enemy. But she was big enough about things to not let her hatred of Parker get in the way of a fledgling friendship with his sister. It was nice to be reasonably minded, she thought.

"Jerome will be our driver today," Valentina said as he ushered them into the Rolls-Royce.

"Oh, yes, I remember you! You're the one who picked us up at the airport," Gisele said.

He nodded to her and waved his hand in the rearview mirror. "Where to, Signora Romeo?"

"First let's do the drive-by tour of the city," she said. "Then we'll go down to the waterfront to do some shopping and have lunch."

And maybe by the time they finished their busy day, old Parker would have boarded a plane back to New York and would be out of her life completely.

"This is the most romantic city I think I've ever seen," Gisele said. "The gorgeous Gothic architecture, all those haunting gargoyles, the tall spires. And oh, everything is bundled up for Christmas, the pine roping everywhere, the twinkly fairy lights. Streetlamps adorned with Christmas wreaths and large red bows. Even the horses pulling carriages down the boulevard are wearing red velvet blankets trimmed in white. It's magical."

Valentina smiled. It was fun seeing this place through fresh eyes. It really was a romantic city, all cozy and warm despite the chill in the air. All the restaurants and bars had warming fireplaces as well, and it was hard to not feel the embrace of seasonal cheer.

"I love being able to show it to you," she said. "The

National Gallery of Art, where the pre-wedding gala dinner will be held, and the Cathedral of *Santo Giacomo il Maggiore*, the site, of course, of the wedding. This place is so steeped in history. But now we eat and shop. Jerome, if you could take us down to the waterfront, please."

They pulled up on the main street in the historic district of Porto Castello, and Jerome let them out to stroll. The street was lined with charming, candy-colored-timbered Alpine farmhouse-style structures with gingerbread wood tracery that made them look as if from a fairy tale. Pine garland was draped along the buildings, and the ubiquitous fairy lights decorated each one as well. Behind the buildings loomed the mighty Alps, and before them stood the Mediterranean Sea. In a nearby marina, beautiful sailboats bobbed in the water, waiting for warmer days to explore the many nearby coves. The church bells from the Cathedral of *Santo Giacomo il Maggiore* began to peal at the top of the hour.

"There's a cozy little pub where we can tuck in and grab some lunch. It's my favorite place on a cold winter's day."

They walked a half block to the King's Arms Tavern and entered into the somewhat dimly lit pub, a blazing fireplace on one side and a long oak bar on the other. They sank into leather club chairs at a small table that was made of a wine cask, and the waitress handed them menus and asked for their drink orders.

"I believe hot chocolate is in order," Valentina said, nodding to her guest. "Sound good to you?"

"Sounds perfect," Gisele said, opening her menu to peruse her choices.

"They make a divine chicken pot pie with a puff pastry

topping," Valentina said. "As well as a beef goulash that'll knock your socks off. I'm game for splitting one of each if you are."

"I'd like nothing better," Gisele said, closing her menu.

The waitress brought their hot cocoa with homemade marshmallows, and they both held them tight to warm their cold hands as they placed their orders.

"So," Valentina said. "Tell me more about you. What do you do back home? How is it that you came to be here for this wedding?"

"I'm an assistant to a production assistant with a production company back home," Gisele said. "In other words, I get sent out to Starbucks about ten times a day to retrieve coffee for the higher-ups. Hardly a glamorous job."

"You have to start somewhere."

"That's true. And I hope eventually to get into the production end of things myself. Right now I'm just soaking it all in, staying late many nights, called in on weekends at the whim of someone above me who likes to make us work just because they can."

"Ahhh, the power plays," she said. "Don't you hate that?"

Gisele nodded. "I'm trying to understand that from a sociological perspective, but so far it's not working. Like why do those higher on the pecking order try to make life so miserable for those on the bottom? So instead I just paste on a smile and hope for the best," she said. "And as far as why I'm here? I'm my brother's date, which I was more than happy to do to go to a royal wedding. What about you? What do you do?"

Valentina shrugged. "I've been at loose ends for a little while. Technically I work with my family's vineyard, though to be truthful I don't have a specific job I can lay claim to. We had a big project I helped to oversee the decorating of, but now that it's done, I'm trying to figure out how to parlay that into something more."

"Sounds fun."

"It was, but in Italy everyone has great design sense. So it's hard to break into the market, there are so many entrenched companies. That said, I could and should use my family connections. I guess I'm just reluctant to do that because I want to succeed on my own."

"That's an admirable quality," her friend said. "But maybe you can use your name to get your foot in the door and then the rest is all from you."

"You're right. It's on my to-do list." She laughed. "I guess I'm pretty lousy at marketing myself, aren't I?"

"We can't all be good at everything," Gisele said. "So dare I ask the million-dollar question?"

Valentina frowned. "Must you?"

She nodded. "I'm afraid so," she said. "After all, I sort of stuck myself in the middle of things. It's the least I can do to educate myself about what I'm trapped in."

Valentina heaved a sigh. "I sure never thought I'd be regaling anyone with this embarrassing story, especially not to the guy's own sister. You must have some magical ways with you, Gisele, to get me to talk."

"In that case, truth serum is definitely called for."

Gisele flagged the waitress down and ordered two shots of tequila, which were delivered in short order. She held up her shot glass to her new friend's glass and smiled. "On the count of three…"

Valentina had a sneaking suspicion she was going to live to regret this. *So much for her good deed for the day*, she thought as she threw back the bitter liquid, squinting her eyes against the strong taste.

"Waitress!" Gisele called, ordering up another shot, priming Valentina to spill her guts.

Oh well, Valentina thought with a grimace. *Here's to being a fool.*

Chapter Ten

"YOU have to understand," Valentina said, her tongue tripping over itself just the teeniest bit. After all, she'd just finished her second shot and she was so not used to drinking tequila. "I'd made such a fool of myself. It was mortifying. And then he cut me off just like that." She tried to snap but her fingers didn't coordinate precisely enough, so it made more of a wispy sound.

"But that was so long ago," Gisele said. "You were just a kid. And he was a college student. If you ask me, he did the right thing. I mean seriously, it would be sort of creepy if he'd hit on you when you were that young."

"But, but, but—"

"I know it was embarrassing. Hey, who hasn't had some humiliating experience with a friend of their big brother's? Mine was with this guy Jeff who was vice president of the student body at their boarding school when Parker was president. Jeff came home to spend Christmas with us. It was the last year my mother was alive—I'll never forget it. It was the best Christmas ever, until I told Jeff that I loved him and he laughed at me. He *laughed* at me! After I confessed my deepest, darkest feelings to him."

"I'm sorry you lost your mamma," Valentina said,

frowning. "That must have been horrible."

"Unimaginable," Gisele said, her eyes getting a far-off look in them. "Something you never really get over."

Valentina placed her hand atop Gisele's. "I wish there was something I could do—"

Gisele held her hands up. "It's been a while. I've had time to adjust. But it did make me treasure each day I have. Which is why I make sure to love my brother with all my heart, cherish those around me, and act like a completely giddy newbie idiot when I get to attend a royal wedding." She grinned.

"And your father?" Valentina was almost afraid to ask since she'd dragged them down so much by broaching the subject of her mother as it was.

Gisele rolled her eyes and shook her head. "My father left my mother years ago," she said. "And when he left her, he left us. He was the bon vivant, the life of the party. He was very flirtatious, and it turns out that he was even more than that—he'd been having affairs all over the place behind my mother's back. Eventually he decided he'd rather be with some woman half his age than with mom and us, and he left." She frowned. "The irony of that is they eventually had children, so here he is a shitty father all over again to a new set of kids. I'd almost pity them if I didn't resent them so much. But of course I can't resent them, because it's not their fault. And really, should I resent them because they get my father and we don't? Because it's not as if he was a worthwhile one anyhow. But since he's the only blood relative left for us, well, I guess it would have been a nice option. But really, we consider him dead, he's that far out of our lives at this point."

"Well, I can certainly relate to not having a father, but

not because he was a bad one, but rather because we lost him too young," Valentina said. "I miss him all the time. But he was a marvelous father. He left very large shoes to fill. Luckily with so many of us combined we've been able to take up the slack, at least in the running of Romeo Wines. But it's never the same."

"Parker does an amazing job trying to be a mother and father to me," Gisele said. "Of course it's impossible for him to be either, and I try to encourage him to take the pressure off himself, but Parker's good at placing high expectations on his own shoulders. But I'm sure with our experience, having had our father betray us as he did, it would be near impossible for him to ever make such a grandiose commitment with a woman. He'd be afraid that at some point his feelings would die, and he'd never want the burden of guilt for having given up."

"Who says you give up?" Valentina flagged the waitress for two more shots. "The idea is you make a commitment and stick to it. It's not optional. It's forever."

The waitress placed the shots in front of them and they threw them back, their eyes watering.

"Well, well, well," a voice came from behind Valentina. "Day-drinking, are we?"

Valentina turned to see one of her brothers hovering over her. She jumped up. "Tomasso! What are you doing here? I thought you weren't even coming to the wedding! And now you're here days early. What gives?"

He shrugged. "I had a lead on a job in the States, but it turns out they don't need me for a few weeks. I could have hung out in New York, but who wants to be alone for Christmas when I could be back for Mamma's cooking instead?" He rubbed his belly for emphasis.

"Lucky me then, as now I can share in this joyous occasion with one of my favorite brothers."

"One of? That doesn't give me too much confidence considering there are six of us."

"You know I can't decide something like that. I love you each for your own special attributes." She gave him a hug. "Oh, and I'd love for you to meet my new friend, Gisele."

Gisele rose on wobbly legs to shake his hand, nearly tipping over. Tomasso caught her just in time and righted her.

"My savior!" she said with a giggle, grabbing the back of the chair for support.

He shook his head. "I don't know about you, but my sister isn't one to get visibly drunk at, hmmm—" He looked at his watch. "At two in the afternoon. You must be a particularly bad influence on her."

Gisele held up her hands defensively. "No! You've got it all wrong. We just shared a few friendly shots of tequila. A social lubricant of sorts."

He arched his brow. "You needed to be lubricated?" he said to his sister with a laugh.

"No. I needed to be inebriated." She slapped her leg and laughed out loud. "That was a great joke! Get it?"

"I'm afraid I need to get you two ladies back to the palace before you find yourselves in trouble."

He held up his hand to attract the waitress's attention and asked for the check.

"But we're having so much fun." Gisele thrust out her bottom lip in a faux pout. "And we were just getting to the good part."

"There was a good part to this?"

"It was the part where Valentina realizes that Parker's a good guy."

He tipped his head toward his sister. "Do tell, sis."

Valentina held her finger up to her lips and shushed Gisele. The last thing she needed was her brother knowing anything about her humiliation at the hands of Parker the Big Fat Jerk Hornsby. Even if he did look so damned hot last night in that suit of his. Especially because of that.

Gisele squinted her eyes, scrunched up her nose and grimaced, apologizing for opening up that can of worms.

"Disregard that line of conversation," she said. "It's my secret." She pretended to lock her lips and throw away an invisible key. "Our secret, that is."

"On second thought, perhaps I should buy you two another round so I can be in on the top-secret conversation. I'm sure it's something I could use against Valentina down the road."

"Oh, look!" Valentina said. "It's Jerome. Come to save me just in the nick of time."

"Probably just as well," Tomasso said. "I think you two are going to need to sleep it off a bit before the reception at Adrian's this evening."

Valentina knit her brows. Crap, there was a big party at Adrian's tonight. Which meant two things: she was now going to be hungover by party time, and she was going to have to partake in the hair of the dog so as to avoid that very thing.

It was going to be a long night.

Chapter Eleven

GISELE returned to the palace apartment in a surprisingly drunk state for it only being near three in the afternoon.

"Seriously, G?" Parker said when he caught the sour stench of liquor as she belched while greeting him. "I thought the plan was to lie low. Play it cool. Definitely not get completely pissed—with, I might add, the woman who would most love to see me splattered over a highway—and stagger home in the middle of the afternoon like you were the town drunk!"

"I resemble that," Gisele said, laughing.

"Seriously, Gisele. I am shocked that you went out and got trashed like this. It's so not like you. What is going on?"

"I was just trying to help," she said as she plunked herself down on the soft leather sofa. "I didn't want my brother to have to suffer in silence."

Parker pinched the bridge of his nose. "Please don't tell me you brought me up in conversation."

She shook her head. "Of course not. Well, not exactly."

"Not exactly? What the hell is that supposed to mean?"

"Well, like, I didn't tell Valentina that you think she's beautiful or anything like that."

"Who says I think she is anyhow?" he said, feeling a vein throbbing in his temple. "And even if I did, who authorized you to discuss it with her?"

"See, I *knew* you think she's gorgeous!"

"I never said any such thing!"

"But you thought it."

"And how might you know that, O omniscient one? Were you peering into your crystal ball or something?"

She shook her head. "I could just tell by the way you looked at her. Like you needed to tuck your tongue back into your mouth or something. Figuratively of course."

Parker began to pace the living room floor. "Please tell me you didn't say that to her."

"Of course not! I wouldn't betray your confidence!"

"I haven't even confided anything in you for you to betray!"

"Yes, but we women know these things."

"Oho. That's rich," he said. "Now you're the all-knowing female who can peer into the minds of men? I swear to you, Gisele, if you've made things worse between me and that woman, I am going to frog-march you onto the next flight home."

Which sounded fine and good except that he heard a loud snort and looked down to see that his sister had fallen fast asleep on the leather couch, a trail of drool leaking from the corner of her mouth onto the kid-soft leather furniture. She never even heard his hollow threat.

Parker heaved a sigh and reached for a cashmere throw draped across the couch and tucked it around Gisele so she'd be more comfortable.

Ugh. He couldn't wait to deal with his sister's new best friend tonight, not knowing what she'd revealed to the woman today. No doubt Valentina was preparing for the palace guards to lead him off to the guillotine for whatever it was he didn't even say to begin with.

The palace had arranged for buses to transport guests to Prince Adrian and Princess Emma's country home outside the city.

Gisele, looking a little green around the gills, parked herself next to Valentina on the bus, leaving Parker to chat up Valentina's brother Tomasso. Clearly his warning to his sister to steer clear of Valentina had fallen on deaf ears.

"So, Tomasso," Parker said, shaking his head. "Long time no see. I hear you intervened this afternoon with our two sisters who were in the tank. I suppose thanks are in order for having precluded all sorts of embarrassing behavior from Gisele had she been left to her own devices."

"Are you kidding? I was more worried about Valentina. She'd have been up on the bar doing belly shots if I hadn't gotten them the hell out of there."

Crap. The idea of licking shots off the flat, sexy belly of a mostly naked Valentina Romeo made Parker's pants instantly grow tighter. How did he continually find himself in these awkward situations and not of his own accord? At least it was dark in the bus; by the time they arrived, hopefully his uninvited erection would have calmed down.

"She does that often then?" Parker said with more

than a hint of wishful thinking in his voice.

Tomasso cocked an eyebrow. "Uh, she better not. But with her, the sky's the limit if she gets in a carousing mood. Valentina does love to be the life of the party."

Parker was tempted to challenge her brother on that allegation; so far all he'd seen was her unpleasant side, and it was hard for him to imagine her being the vivacious bon vivant. It was hard to say though. As a young teenager, Valentina was a lot of fun, at least when it came to things like playing sports. But looking at her now, the idea of any sort of athletic pursuit with her inevitably led down the path of his needing to get his mind out of the gutter.

He sure hoped Valentina was as hungover as his sister was because at least then she'd likely not have the energy to castigate him for breathing the wrong way or daring to look at her at the party tonight. With any luck, the place was big enough for the two of them to avoid each other altogether.

The bus pulled past a guardhouse flanked by tall brick walls that were draped with holly and pine roping entwined with white lights. It continued along a tree-lined driveway for nearly a mile until they came upon Adrian's home. As future king of Monaforte, Adrian would be entitled to a palatial country home naturally. But wow, was this place ever a huge. Parker had been told the two-story Georgian-style brick home contained sixteen rooms. A quick glance at the roofline revealed eight chimneys. At least you could stay warm in a place like this.

The guests deboarded the bus and followed the slate walkway to the oversized front double doors hung with two enormous Christmas wreaths. A butler opened the door to allow the guests in, and others quickly took guests' coats and directed everyone to drinks and appetizers being passed. Parker spotted Luca and made a beeline to him while grabbing a glass of wine from a passing tray.

"Parker!" Luca said. "Enjoying yourself, I trust?"

Parker held up his glass. "Even more now," he said, hoping that came across as a joke even though deep down he was sort of serious. This day was making him want to drink to forget. "What a spread your brother's got going here."

"It's spectacular, isn't it? The firstborn has all the luck."

Parker shrugged. "Yeah, not too shabby. I'd settle for it. Although minus his responsibilities."

They both laughed.

"I'll drink to that. So, things go well with Valentina last night?" Luca said, arching an eyebrow in curiosity.

"Um, I suppose." Parker cocked his own brow, wondering what Luca meant by that comment. This was getting weird: he'd never been in a dueling eyebrow conversation before.

"I just thought maybe you and she might, well, enjoy each other's company a bit." Luca raised his other brow.

What the fuck?

Parker decided to furrow his instead. "The thing is, Luca, it's just that, well, you see, um—"

"Well, look who it is!" Gisele ran up to Luca and gave him a big hug. So much for royal protocol.

"Little G! What's up, my honorary little sister?" Luca said, obviously unconcerned with her breach in diplomatic behavior and giving her a huge squeeze back. "So glad your brother brought you along. Tell me what you've done since you've been here."

Parker threw her a dirty look, as in *ix-nay on the equila-*

tay inge-bay.

"Ohmigod, Valentina and I had such a great day. She took me all around the city, and we saw the famous landmarks, and then we went to this great pub for lunch, and I made her drink truth serum—"

"Truth serum?"

"That's what my sorority sisters called it when we did shots of tequila. I find tequila has unique properties to make the consumer say and do really remarkable things. Kind of encourages you to let your hair down."

Luca nodded his head slowly. "You don't say…" He looked at Parker, suppressing a laugh. "And did you find my cousin let her hair down at all?"

"Well… she was starting to, but then Tomasso showed up and put an end to that—"

"And then my little sister took a much-needed nap upon her return to the palace." Parker winked at Luca as he placed his hands on Gisele's shoulders, trying to steer her away.

"Oh, and speak of the hungover devil," Luca said, reaching for Valentina's hand and pulling her toward their conversation. "I understand you and Gisele got a chance to paint the town red today."

Valentina rubbed her temples. "I'm not sure if there was any painting going on. More like swilling."

"Swilling?" her cousin said.

"It sounded like such a good idea at the time," Valentina said. "But now I'm afraid the only way I'm going to last through this party is with the hair of the dog."

"In which case," Luca said, reaching for a passing tray of champagne and pulling off two flutes, one for Valentina and one for Gisele, "bottoms up, ladies."

He and Parker exchanged glances and grinned. Finally things were picking up for Parker, starting with Luca's evil retribution on his cousin. He was going to enjoy watching her suffer for the rest of the evening. And she'd be lucky if he didn't go find some pots and pans from the kitchen and bang them right up against her ears just for the sheer enjoyment of it. If she wanted to play mean, he could too.

Only thing was, why did it feel unkind to even think that way?

Chapter Twelve

VALENTINA felt like a herd of elephants had stampeded overtop her head. She was not a drinker really. Of course she drank wine—that went without saying for a Romeo. Her family of vintners was all about wine. But tequila? She could have counted on one hand how many times she'd even had it served to her in a drink in her whole life, and never in shots.

What was she thinking, throwing that stuff back like it was mother's milk? Just because it was clear didn't mean it was harmless. Nail polish remover was clear too, but she wouldn't suck that down her gullet. She needed to remember that mantra next time. But there would not be a next time—she was so not going to indulge in tequila shots ever again. She made a mental note to avoid Mexican holidays just in case the temptation lurked.

She'd boarded the bus for the party and sat next to her partner in crime, Gisele, hoping she'd feel better with someone who likely felt equally hungover. After all, misery did love company, right? But then the brother boarded the bus. And parked his butt—his delicious-looking butt—right smack-dab in front of her. He had on some cologne that should have made her want to throw up but instead had her yearning to bury her nose in the crook of his neck and just inhale the aroma. While twirling her fingers through his straight-from-the beach blond hair.

It was a sort of oaky, woodsy, hike-in-the-mountains-followed-by-crazy-good-sex-on-a-bed-of-pine-needles scent. Not that she'd ever had sex—good or bad—on a bed of pine needles. But if she did, she knew it would smell just like him. Which was making her crazy because she so did not want to think good thoughts about the scent of Parker Hornsby or how her hands would fit just so over the curve of his perfectly shaped ass or how, in another world—one in which she hadn't licked wounds caused by him for years—she'd give strong consideration to jumping the man's bones right here, right on the bus, were it not for royal protocol, which of course she had to adhere to, what with it being her cousin's wedding after all.

When Parker was leaning toward Tomasso, engrossed in conversation, Valentina discreetly inched her hand over the edge of his seat-back and touched his coat. Yeah, yeah, that sounded sort of weird. But she'd noticed it when they were in line to board the bus. It was a black camel-hair topcoat and it fit him so well, and it looked so soft and inviting and sort of well-loved. She wanted to stroke her hands over it for just a minute, just to prove to herself that it couldn't feel as amazing as she thought it would.

But she was wrong. It felt even better. And maybe it was because filling it out was one entirely hot piece of man, one she outwardly detested but if she were to be honest with herself, she'd have to admit that old feelings might be harder to kill off than she'd hoped. Because all she could think of was how it would feel to wrap herself around him in that coat. And then slowly, with great deliberation, unbutton it, slip it from his strong shoulders, then run her hands down the crisply pressed field of his sexy blue dress shirt, fondling his strong pectoral muscles, stroking her hands down the length of his cut stomach, which would eventually lead to one of her favorite parts of a man's body: that happy trail, the beacon that led inexorably to where she wanted to go.

Of course she knew the road to perdition was paved with that very sexy trail of hair she even now could recall ogling all those years ago when Parker wore his swim trunks at the beach. Or went shirtless while playing football, sweat dripping down his belly just there in that perfect spot. Back then she hadn't a true clue what exactly that led to, but now, good Lord, she had a gunnysack of ideas about what she could do at the end of that goody trail. Talk about a pot of gold at the end of the rainbow...

Valentina closed her eyes, imagining what it would be like just to ease her hand beneath the waistband of his suit pants. She wouldn't bother taking the time to undo his belt buckle or even unzip his fly. She'd be too impatient to get to the goods. And now she even had an inkling how good those goods were: when he'd tried to save her from falling at the table last night, he'd pressed up against her just so, and suffice it to say it did indeed rescue her. And fueled her vivid dreams last night as well. Shame she was such a stubborn thing, because otherwise she could have just gotten things rolling with that very hip-to-hip introduction and by now they'd be kicking back and smoking a Camel.

But alas, about as close as she was going to let herself get to Parker Hornsby would be copping a feel of his soft overcoat, not whatever might be hard beneath his undergarments, darn it.

Parker turned to say something his sister, snagging

Valentina's fingers in the collar of his coat. He cocked his head toward her, a look of confusion on his face.

"Trying to choke me with my own clothing now?" He smirked at her.

Valentina pulled her hand away as if she'd touched a hot stove.

"Go away," she said, embarrassed she couldn't compose a better comeback than that but glad she had at least deflected the fact that she'd been creeping on his coat.

"Trust me, Valentina, if I could, I would," he said, his lips pursed together. "You've made it abundantly clear I'm not welcome in your little slice of the universe. And I'm doing my best to steer clear of you. But I'm here for Luca, and you're just going to have to deal with that."

Valentina was so glad it was dark in the bus because a flush of embarrassment had no doubt stained her cheeks a bright red. She didn't know what was wrong with her, why she couldn't bring herself to act in a civil manner around this man. All she knew was something about Parker Hornsby caused her to revert to behaving like an idiotic, awkward teenager, and it was making her crazy.

True to her word, Valentina capitalized on the free-flowing champagne and the multitude of toasts and managed to tamp down her hangover with the aid of a slight alcohol infusion into her bloodstream. Amazing how that worked. Eventually she slipped upstairs to the family quarters to find a bathroom to use, having tired of bathroom lines in the downstairs powder rooms.

As she came out of the bathroom, she noticed a sitting room where coats had been hung on several racks lined up side by side. There weren't many left as buses had been transferring guests back to town for the past hour or so, and many guests had already departed. She flicked on the light and slipped into the room, making a beeline to the coats. Sliding the hangers down one by one, she shifted the garments until she found the one she was looking for.

She pulled it from the hanger and held the collar up to her nose, inhaling the scent. She moaned. God, she was going to need to do something about this weird need to have some contact with that man. But not quite yet. Because the coat felt so warm and soft in her hands and she started thinking about how wonderful it would feel if she could just wrap herself up in it and maybe close her eyes for a few minutes while she thought about the finer points of Parker Hornsby (disregarding all the jerky ones, which she knew were there somewhere). Only this room was lacking a bed, which sounded really perfectly comfortable right about now.

She listened for the sound of any potential people approaching. The last she'd spied Parker downstairs, he'd seemed pretty engrossed in a conversation with a count from some far-flung country in Eastern Europe. Surely that meant he'd remain downstairs for a good long while still.

She grabbed Parker's topcoat and slipped out the door, turning off the light behind her. She approached the very next door she found and, turning the knob, found herself in a lovely room with a large, soft bed and no one there to bother her. She slipped off her shoes and settled herself onto the bed, tucking Parker's soft coat around her, a makeshift security blanket of sorts, and she drifted off to sleep thinking about the previous occupant of that coat and how good it would feel if it were him and not his outerwear she was pressed up against.

In her dreams she nuzzled up to Parker, mashing her body to his like a puppy finding a cozy spot atop a pile of his littermates. Not even a tiny bit of space between bodies, all warmth and snuggling and hard body up against hers. She knew it was a bad idea, but she couldn't help herself— her hands kept reaching for his body, the feel of his hard chest, and even harder parts farther down. She wasn't sure if she moaned in her sleep or out loud, but she turned over and drifted off again, secure in the knowledge that no one would find her here.

Chapter Thirteen

IT was late and Parker was ready to get back to the palace. He really didn't want to wait for the next shuttle back, so he was about to order an Uber, but first had to retrieve his coat. It was too cold outside to leave that behind; with heavy snow in the forecast he was going to need it all week long.

He mounted the steps to the family wing of the estate. Luca told him he thought he'd find his coat in the room that was the second or third door on the right down the right-hand hallway. He hoped it would be where it was supposed to be so he wouldn't walk in on anyone doing God knows what. It was so quiet upstairs; amazing how these old homes were so soundproofed you could hear nothing, even with a large crowd right downstairs.

He found the second door closed and he tapped lightly on it, just to be sure he wasn't intruding on anyone. He opened the door, which creaked quietly as he entered the darkened room. Weird, he'd thought he'd find the room with racks of coats lined up, but there seemed to be nothing of the sort. As his eyes adjusted to the darkness, he noticed someone appeared to be sound asleep on the bed. God, he needed to slip out and fast; clearly he'd gone to the wrong room. But wait—was that his coat covering up whomever was snoring on the bed?

He tiptoed over to the bed and inspected the coat as best he could given the lack of illumination in the room. It was most definitely the long black camel-hair coat that had belonged to his father. He could tell just by the feel of it that it was his; he knew the touch of that from years of his father's wearing it, long before it became his. It was one of the few things his father left behind when he moved out, and Parker treasured it as something good that remained of his father's memories.

He slowly stroked the sleeve of the coat, so familiar was he with the touch of the thing it stirred up long-ago memories of sitting alongside his father at church every Sunday when he was young, tucked securely in the safe umbrella of his arms, stroking his tiny fingers along it as if it was a small child's blankie. His hands came to the leather dome-woven buttons at the base of the sleeve just as he heard a woman groan, and he jumped back.

"Do it again," the woman's voice said.

He tried to make out in the dark who was talking to him, but still he couldn't see.

"Do what again?" he said. What a strange thing that he was even asking that of someone who was lying there wrapped in his father's vintage coat. He should just demand it back and leave.

"Stroke my arm the way you just did," she said. "It felt good. Very sensual."

Okay then. Whatever. While he was certain nothing good could come of this, what was he to do? So he slowly dragged his fingers down the sleeve again, taking a minute to enjoy the sensation of the soft camel hair on his fingertips.

Just then a hand reached out and began to stroke his arm slowly, softly. He got chill bumps.

"Does that feel good?" the voice said.

He nodded. But of course the person wouldn't even know he'd done that.

"Of… of course," he said, stammering.

Then he felt the hand slide up his abdomen, across his chest, and, *helllloooo,* what the hell was going on here?

"Does that feel even better?" she said.

And he wanted to tell her no but that would be lying, and while he had no idea what was going on, somehow he was unable to drag himself away from whatever it was. Whether it was his curiosity or his seemingly chronic state of horniness that had vexed him ever since he'd laid eyes on that cursed Valentina Romeo… Damn, he needed a cold shower.

Aaaannnnd that wasn't going to happen because that soft hand was now stroking across his crotch, featherlight, but it didn't take more than a feather to turn that thing into a tool that was hard as steel, and his breathing quickly became labored.

"What are you doing?" he said, dying to know who this person was. "And who are you?"

He wanted nothing more than to reach over and reciprocate, place his hands on this strange woman's most intimate spots as well, but he couldn't do that, not without knowing who she was and what she was up to.

"Listen," he said, pressing himself to her hand even as he knew he had to not do that. "As amazing as this feels, we have to stop. I don't even know who you are."

"Pretty please," she said, pressing harder, giving his cock a squeeze. "For me, Parker?"

Parker? Whoever this was knew him. But he hardly knew anyone at this party.

"Why don't you let me have my coat? And if you want, I can call for a ride home for you."

"But first kiss me. I want to feel your mouth on mine, Parker."

Parker's eyes widened. Should he? She knew who he was. But this seemed all wrong. But her hand was pressed to his crotch, and she wasn't showing signs of stopping.

He leaned over, unable to make out whose face it was. "Who are you and how do you know my name?"

"Huh?" she said, her voice sounding distant. Her hands came to rest, unmoving, right on top of his very swollen cock. Parker thought he could die. And then he heard snoring.

"I'm sorry, Miss… whoever you are," he said, reaching for the coat and gently nudging her shoulder. "Wake up."

The woman muttered something and rolled over so she was facing him. He leaned down so his face was close to hers, trying to make out who it might be. He gasped.

"Valentina?" he said, perhaps a little too loudly. "What are you doing in my coat?"

"You?" she said, her voice suddenly shrill. "What are you doing to me?"

"Me? Doing to you? More like what are you doing to me?" He stepped back. "You were talking to me. I didn't even know who you were. You rubbed your hands up against me. You asked me to kiss you."

"I did no such thing!" She rolled over on the bed to create distance between them.

"Are you kidding me?" he said. "I came in here to get my coat. Just minding my business, ready to leave. I just needed my coat. And I come up here to find you curled up in it and, and, well, I don't know what you were thinking. But I do know you called out to me. You asked me to kiss you."

Valentina climbed out of the bed, grabbed her shoes, and stood face-to-face with him. "I would no sooner ask you to kiss me than I would, well, than I would choose to kiss you myself."

Parker smiled. "Oh, really?"

"Yes, really."

"How do you know what you don't want when you've never even tried it?"

She glared at him in the dark room. "Trust me, that I can live without."

He arched his brow. "You said yourself that you wanted me to kiss you. I think I owe it to you to give you a taste of what you're missing out on. And you owe it to yourself to give it a try."

With that, he lowered his lips to hers, placing his hands softly on her waist and pulling her toward him. He knew he had to tread lightly, like trying to trap a cornered animal. Calm words and gentle motions were in order. He ever so softly traced a path along the seam of her lips, coaxing her to open them to him.

"There," he said between soft licks. "That's not so bad, now is it?"

He pulled her slightly closer, his hips pressed to hers so she wouldn't be able to mistake how she was making him feel.

"I know you want me, Valentina," he said. "I'm yours for the taking, baby. Go on, just give it a try. If you decide it's not for you, then we can call it a night."

His hand reached up to the back of her head, angling her head just so, giving him the right position to again place his mouth over hers, pressing his tongue to part her lips, which he could tell were relaxing into his kiss.

"That's it, baby," he said, and before he knew it her tongue had joined in the fun, tangling with his, stroking along his licks. She let out a moan that caused him to pull her closer, rubbing his cock to her pelvis. He groaned.

In the darkened room they were far from the bustle of the party downstairs; they couldn't even hear the music playing or the din of conversation. All they could hear was the chorus of moans and panting breath as the two of them grappled with one another. Valentina tugged on his shirt, pulling it loose from the confines of his belted pants, and she slid her hands up and under his shirt and over his chest, moaning aloud once more. Parker slipped the metallic strap of her cocktail dress down past her shoulder, exposing her breast for his pleasure. He took a chance in separating from her mouth so he could lick his way toward her breast, finally finding a hard nipple that he pulled into his warm mouth.

Meanwhile, Valentina's hand had worked its way beneath the waistband of Parker's pants, impatiently fumbling with the button and zipper, mercifully freeing his erection from the prison it had been contained in. Parker's mouth had found its way back to Valentina's as his hand deftly lifted the hem of her body-hugging metallic dress, his fingers sliding beneath her skimpy thong and finally just there, right where he needed them to be.

"Oh. My. God," he moaned. "You're so wet."

He pushed her gently against the bed and she fell back against it, and for a minute she began to protest but he pressed a finger to her lips and lowered himself to his knees, spreading her legs apart and planting soft kisses along her thighs as he worked his mouth toward her warm center. One long stroke with his tongue, another, and another and Valentina moaned aloud.

"Oh God, Parker. More." She rocked her hips against his tongue and he pressed first one then two fingers inside her slick center, burying them and pulling back, then pressing farther in, letting her know in no uncertain terms what he wanted to do with another appendage of his just as soon as he made sure she was satisfied. He dragged his tongue over her clit, drawing masterful circles around it. She pumped madly against him.

"Right there, oh, shit, Parker, God, fuck!"

He could feel her climax rolling through her, her muscles clamping on his fingers as her body shuddered under his efforts. He held her as her orgasm settled down and she remained quiet, breathing heavily.

Parker climbed up on the bed so they were side by side and took her mouth with his as she licked his wet lips and reached for his desperate cock. He groaned.

"I need to be in you so badly," he said in a whisper.

"I don't have any protection," she said. "Do you?"

Parker mentally rolled his eyes. How the hell could he have failed to have anything with him? Crap. It had been so long since he'd even used condoms—he and Amanda had gotten past that stage long ago—and he hadn't thought to restock his wallet. And the last thing he'd expected at Luca's wedding was this, of all things.

He shook his head no, but Valentina clearly had a plan B, so she wrapped her fingers around his hard cock and worked her hand up and down, first slowly but then in an increasingly fast rhythm, rolling her hand over the head and then down again, then sliding her other hand to cup his balls.

"I'm not gonna last long," he said, thrusting himself toward her hand as his voracious mouth searched for her breast again. He dragged his tongue across a nipple and blew on it, marveling at how it hardened so readily, and then he fastened his lips over her wet nipple and sucked as she pulled on him until he could feel it building and building until at last with a loud groan he stilled, then came in her hand as she gentled his cock and he spilled his seed on her hands and his belly.

They lay there for a long moment, not talking, just breathing hard.

And for a fleeting moment Parker thought that perhaps Berlin Wall had finally been torn down, that they had made some real progress tonight and maybe he could even raid one of Luca's brothers' apartments in search of a mega box of condoms so that they could continue this little diversion once back at the palace.

"Knock, knock," a voice shouted from the door.

"Oh, shit," Parker said, splayed out as he was with his pants undone and his come still wet on his stomach, not to mention on Valentina's hands. He grabbed Valentina's strap and tugged it back up over her shoulder, helped her pull her dress down over her panties, and he dove over the far edge of the bed, tossing his top coat back on top of her as he did. He lay down on the ground, trying to get the comforter to cover him in the event someone could see to that side of the bed in the dark.

"Is anybody in here?" The person switched on a light.

Parker didn't recognize the voice immediately.

Valentina feigned as if she'd been asleep and stirred. "Who's there?"

"It's Emma. Val, is that you?" Emma—Prince Adrian's wife, the hostess of the evening.

"Oh no!" Valentina said. "I must have fallen asleep."

"Sure looks like you did," Emma said. "How'd you end up here?"

"I came upstairs to use the bathroom and then I went to find my coat and I must have mistaken this for mine," she said. "And I guess I was just so sleepy that I slipped in here to take a little catnap."

Emma laughed. "Well, that is certainly a strange thing to do at a party, but to each his own. The party's winding down, so you might want to get down there before the shuttle stops running."

"Right," Valentina said. "Thanks for the heads-up."

Parker listened for Emma's footsteps to retreat before he finally emerged from beneath the fall of the comforter. He reached for Valentina, trying to pull her close to him. But she was scurrying to get out of the bed, throwing his coat toward him.

"You might want to cover up with that or people will know what we've been up to," she said.

"I don't care if anyone knows. Do you?"

She squinted at him in the dim light. "Are you kidding me?" She shook her head as she wrung her hands. "No one can ever know about this, Parker. This was a huge mistake on my part. I don't know what I was thinking. You caught me at a particularly weak moment. But trust me: never again. Ever."

With that she reached for a tissue on the nightstand and cleaned off her fingers, grabbed her silver pumps that

Jenny Gardiner

she'd left by the bed, and stormed out of the room without a glance back.

Chapter Fourteen

VALENTINA was plunged headlong into a psychological walk of shame.

Sure, she might not be trotting around in broad daylight wearing sky-high stilettos and a skirt wedged up to her wazoo, last night's mascara smeared beneath her eyes in a tattoo of guilt, but yeah, she was pretty appalled at her actions from the night before and at her inability to maintain at least a modicum of self-control. Not to mention that she'd done more with Parker in less time than she ever had with her last however-many boyfriends.

She must've set some sort of land-speed record, and not in a good way. Well, maybe in a good way, only not with him. If she weren't so damned mortified, she'd almost marvel how one could transform from mortal enemies to near-lovers in, oh, the blink of an eye. And enjoy it so much.

And yet she was going to have to pull up her big-girl panties and show up today and feign indifference and not let on to the world that she'd had her hands on Parker's privates and oh God, *she'd had her hands on Parker's privates!*

If she even had someone to admit this to, they'd never believe it. But she wasn't going to breathe a word anyhow because, well, nothing good would come of it. She would be the laughingstock of her brothers for the rest of eternity, for one thing. Luca would about wet his pants guffawing over it, for another. And all of a sudden the attention of the wedding of the year would divert from royal grandeur to Little Miss Can't Keep Your Hands to Yourself, who still didn't quite know how she'd gone from diverting to an upstairs bathroom for a quick pee break to practically mauling Parker Hornsby—after he masterfully satisfied her with his talented mouth—on her cousin's guest bed.

If it was even a guest bed—she didn't even know where she'd been—and not just some random room. One that mercifully was unoccupied and, well, crap, now came the part where she had to admit to herself that wowza, that was a seriously smokin'-hot sexual encounter of the best kind. Shame it was with the one man on the planet who was completely and totally off-limits for all eternity.

Because if he wasn't, she might just sign on the dotted line for at least a command performance, if not more. And she sure as hell would be running out to the nearest *farmacia* condom vending machine to stock up for a long winter's rest (although on second thought, maybe not so much rest).

Maybe she'd been on to something, pining away for old Parker Hornsby—she should've nicknamed him Parker Horny—all those years ago. Who knew he'd be so skillful with his tongue? And his mouth. And his hands. And his fingers. She could feel the molten heat of both embarrassment and sexual arousal spreading like a lava flow across her flesh.

Okay. She had to pull herself together and make it down to breakfast and pretend that nothing happened. Because after all, nothing *had* happened as far as anyone knew. And she'd deal with Parker by not dealing with Parker. Easy peasy.

If she could have slipped into the room like a spy on a mission, trying to avoid detection, she would have. Unfortunately that wasn't going to happen as the palace was filling with more and more guests by the day. And of course this morning the dining room had none other than Parker and Gisele practically awaiting her arrival.

"Valentina!" Gisele said, reaching over to give her the two-cheek kiss. She was adapting to the local traditions quite nicely. Shame Parker was her brother though. It was much easier when she was having nothing to do with him. Even though she was officially never having anything to do with him. But that's hard to uphold once a man's had his mouth where Parker's was only hours earlier.

Oh God. His ever so talented mouth. There. So. Freaking. Amazing.

Okay, Valentina. Get it together. No more stray thoughts. Focus. You can do it. No need for distractions.

"*Buon giorno*, Valentina," Parker said, reaching over to press a kiss to each of her cheeks. Why was it that it felt so much more intimate coming from him, dammit?

Get it together, Valentina.

Valentina tipped a brisk nod to Parker and turned her attention immediately to his sister.

"What happened to you last night? I tried to find you

and you were gone," she said to Gisele.

Parker's sister darted her eyes suspiciously. "I um, became engrossed in conversation and it got late and the next thing you know, we were on our way back to the palace and I tried to find you but the shuttle bus was leaving and he convinced me you'd be fine on your own—"

Valentina squinted at her friend. "So you came back to the palace with someone? Was it a... boy?" She gave her a pronounced wink. Yay. What better way to divert attention away from her idiocy than by shining a spotlight on someone else's late-night behavior?

Gisele asked a passing butler for a cappuccino.

"No distracting me, now," Valentina said. "'Fess up."

Gisele pursed her lips. "It's sort of awkward."

"Trust me, honey, you don't know awkward." She no sooner said that than she regretted the utterance. A broad grin spread across Parker's face. She threw him the stink-eye and continued. "I mean it's okay, you can tell me. I won't judge."

After all, she was hoping no one would judge her if word got out. Which it wouldn't. But still...

"No really. It wasn't any big deal," Gisele said as the butler handed her the drink and she took a sip of it. "I just got caught up in conversation with your brother is all."

"You'll have to be more specific," Valentina said. "There's practically a soccer team's worth of brothers in my family."

"Well, considering I've only met the one—"

"Tomasso? Sweet Tomasso?" she said. "Oh, that's wonderful. He's one of my favorite brothers."

"But didn't you admit then that all your brothers are

your favorite brothers?"

She nodded. "Yes, it's true. But I have a soft spot in my heart for Tomasso. He and I got into all sorts of trouble when we were little. Our mamma had a special corner in the kitchen where he and I had to sit, nose to nose, each time we got caught, which was practically daily. So, uh, you and my brother then?" She held up her hand and twined her pointer and middle fingers together symbolically.

Gisele shook her head. "It's not like that, really. We just stayed up talking till late. That's all."

If "talking" was gonna be the euphemism for making out like a couple of horny, sex-starved teenagers, well, then, Valentina must've been all talked-out after her encounter of the night prior.

"Well, I think it's awesome that you two have hit it off," Valentina said. "You have my heartfelt approval."

"Thanks," her friend said. "Though not sure if there's anything to approve of. I did find him interesting. But what about you? Where'd you run off to last night?"

There went that rush of red-hot heat racing up her neck and across her face.

"I was around," she said, avoiding eye contact with Parker. "I guess we must have just crossed paths."

Parker's eyes widened. "I found it to be a bit chilly there last night. Didn't you, Valentina?"

She shook her head. "I was perfectly warm." She took a sip of her cappuccino and looked away.

"Oh really," he said. "Because you looked like you could have used an extra jacket or maybe a coat."

She choked on her drink and shot daggers at him. "I was perfectly toasty."

Parker nodded. "Then again, at times you seemed

downright hot. You might want to get that checked out."

Gisele's phone dinged with a text and she got up. "Would you excuse me? I've got a little errand to run."

Parker looked at her in curiosity, his brow furrowed, but then sidled up to Valentina just as she started to slip out of the room. He followed her through the Great Hall and down a corridor that would lead to the servants' quarters. He boxed her into a corner where the hallway took an abrupt turn, his face just inches away from hers.

"You can play hard to get all you want, Valentina, but I know and you know that we both had an amazing time last night," he said, his smile speaking volumes about how amazing that time was. God, it killed her to know that he was thinking back on the very things she was remembering, and he was reflecting fondly while she was cringing (while also getting a little hot and bothered—talk about mixed internal messages).

"Don't flatter yourself, Mr. Hornsby," she said. "I've had better."

Parker leaned over and whispered in her ear. "You are so full of shit your eyes are brown. You know you liked it as much as I did. I don't know who you think you're fooling by pretending that didn't mean anything to you. I was on the receiving end of your mouth, honey—and your hands as well—and I can tell you that wasn't any accident. And if you've had better, well then, lucky you, because that was a-fucking-mazing. And you know it."

God, she hated that he was right. And that she would under other circumstances pay good money for a command performance.

Parker leaned in and, without even giving her a chance to think, took a long, slow swipe along her mouth with his

tongue. "And as soon as you're ready to admit it, you know where to find me."

With that, he turned on his heel and walked back to the dining room, leaving Valentina with a racing heart and some suddenly damp panties. Not quite the way she'd intended to start her day.

Chapter Fifteen

PARKER decided to keep his distance from Valentina for a while to give her time to warm up to him a bit. So far it had been twenty-four torturous hours, and he'd hated every minute of this fledgling woo-her-by-ignoring-her policy. Besides, it had killed him to watch her at the cocktail party in the more intimate Queen's Hall last night, so close but yet so far.

At least it was easier for him to avoid her simply because more family members had arrived and he knew them all, having spent plenty of time with them over the years. And whereas he'd felt some odd imbalance earlier in the week, now he felt like he held a slight upper hand, if only because he had that brief encounter to hold on to and he wanted to believe it actually meant something to Valentina, and once he figured out what was holding her back, maybe they could work on that a bit.

Yet in the meantime. he could only glance at her from the corner of his eye as she threw her head back in a coquettish laugh with that prince from Moldavia or Micronesia or wherever it was he was from. And when her hand settled too comfortably on the forearm of that financier from London she was sharing drinks with, he could only cringe in silence. Or as her smile looked far too sincere when that professional footballer from France was obviously attempting to woo her with his dubious charms, Parker ground his teeth so hard his ears hurt.

The afternoon's schedule was a sleigh ride for family and wedding attendants in the Royal Gardens, a two-hundred-plus-acre park on the edge of the city that contained fields and forests and trails for all sorts of outdoor activities. With heavy snow in the forecast, it promised to be a cold but seasonally festive event.

"*So* cool we're going on a sleigh ride," Gisele said to her brother. "I've never done this before. I don't even know what to wear!"

"I'd say given that they're calling for at least eight inches of snow and the temperatures will be below twenty degrees, something warm would be a good start."

His sister rolled her eyes. "Thanks for the insight. But I'd like to look a little stylish. I mean, if I put a hat on. I'm going to have hat hair and that's the worst."

"Actually I'd say it's way worse if you get frostbite."

"Oh you're full of brilliant observations today," Gisele said. "But seriously, do you think we'll be warm enough?"

"I'm sure they wouldn't do it if we weren't going to be well-cared for," he said. "Not like they're going to leave us for dead, freezing in the woods with wild dogs chasing us."

"Well then, phew. That's a relief." Gisele gathered a pile of outerwear, including thick gloves, a cashmere hat and scarf, and her warmest down jacket. "This is so romantic, like right out of *Doctor Zhivago*."

"Doesn't everyone end up miserable or dead in that story?"

"Okay, grumpy grandpa," she said. "Cheer up! It's going to be a perfect afternoon."

Cheer up, schmeer up. The only way he could imagine it being perfect would be if Valentina gave up the charade and finally decided to play fair. Or really if she'd play at all.

In the plaza at the entrance to the park were a host of two-, four-, and eight-seated sleighs manned by large, strong draft horses. The sleighs were covered in seasonal garlands, and the horses had the requisite sleigh bells attached so that with every move they made it sounded as if Santa would show up at any minute. When it came time to pair off into the sleighs, Parker tried to position himself close to Valentina, hoping Luca and Larkin would remember their promise to link the two of them together for all the wedding festivities. But instead, his darned sister wormed her way up with Valentina, and before he knew it they were both snuggled together atop the leather upholstery of a two-seated sleigh, a fur throw tucked in around their legs, with cups of hot toddies in their hands just like they were an old married couple. What the hell?

He was going to have to have a word with Gisele about thwarting his moves.

When Parker finally climbed into a sleigh, he found he was seated with another of Valentina's brothers, this time Lorenzo. He and Lorenzo had gotten along like siblings back when he visited Luca frequently during college breaks.

"Brotha from another motha," Parker said, reaching out to fist-bump Lorenzo. "What's going on with you?"

Lorenzo pulled a flask from the breast pocket of his jacket. "For now, staying warm with this." He offered a swig to Parker, who gulped it down and squinted his eyes against the strong liquid.

"That's good stuff," he said. "So how's life been treating you?"

"Good," Lorenzo said. "Busy. I was never happier to finish the harvest this year. Anything that could go wrong did. Believe me, if it weren't for this wedding, I'd be heading off somewhere warm to recuperate."

"Yeah," Parker said. "I don't blame you. So, can you believe Luca was the first of us to fall?"

The three young men had hung out together a lot the summer Parker spent with them at the beach.

"It's crazy. I never thought he'd be so foolish."

"Foolish, eh?" Parker said. "I figure at this point it's probably okay to start settling down, no?"

"Not while I have blood coursing through my veins."

Parker smiled. "I gotta give you credit for determination."

"What, like you want to get married?"

Parker shrugged. "Honestly, I haven't given it much thought. Though I don't exactly have that much faith in the female sex these days, not after my last girlfriend hosed me like she did." He proceeded to tell Lorenzo the whole story.

"Dude. No wonder you don't want to get married."

"I thought it was you who didn't want to get married."

"I don't. But hearing that, I'm sure you don't either. I mean, you can't trust them as far as you can throw them."

"There must be at least one reliable, trustworthy woman in the world."

Lorenzo shook his head. "Yeah, like my mom and my sister. That's about it."

"You mean Valentina?" Parker hoped he was completely opaque bringing her up so casually.

"Please," Lorenzo said. "You don't have a thing for her too, do you?"

"I hardly know her," Parker said. "I mean, back in the day, she was fine. But she was just a kid."

Lorenzo slapped him on the back. "God, did she have it bad for you. Following you everywhere like a puppy dog, that desperate look in her eyes."

Parker side-eyed him. "What?"

"There's no way you didn't notice it," he said. "She was pathetically transparent. We all gave her so much shit for it too."

Ahhh… A lone girl with all those brothers. Of course it was even harder for her to risk her feelings on him and for him to then shut her down… Why hadn't he realized that on his own? Because he was a thickheaded young man, that's why.

"Honestly, I hadn't noticed much," he said, lying through his teeth. "But poor Valentina. She must have been mortified."

"Eh, she got over it," he said. "She's had enough boyfriends to show for it."

Parker's face fell. "She has a lot of boyfriends?"

"I can't remember who she's dating now," her brother said. "Some guy named Dante, I think. I don't know any details. Maybe he hired her to decorate his flat in Florence? Or was that Mario Lupetto?"

"Lupetto?" Parker said. "Doesn't that mean 'small wolf'? What's your sister doing dating a guy who's a little

Red Carpet Romeo

wolf? You should protect her from that."

Lorenzo held up his hands. "Hey, I'm not in charge of my sister's love life. I can't even manage my own. If she wants to be with some guy who's a wolf, so be it. But just because his name is that doesn't mean he is, you know."

Parker must've been hallucinating. Of course just because the guy had that name meant nothing. But then why did he suddenly want to go skin that little wolf so he wouldn't sink his bloodthirsty teeth into Valentina?

Chapter Sixteen

AFTER the sleigh rides ended, guests gathered around a bonfire for a short while and toasted the happy couple. Bit by bit, guests boarded the return bus, and just as Valentina was about to get on the last shuttle, she realized her phone must've fallen out during the ride. The drivers had just departed with the sleighs, so she decided to chase hers down so that she was sure to have her phone back before it was ruined by snow.

"I don't think that's a great idea," Gisele said. "It's getting dark and it's really cold. Plus look at how hard it's snowing. I'm sure someone can radio ahead to the driver to find it."

"It's fine," Valentina said. "They just went down this path—they can't have gone very far—it's a bunch of sleighs and horses. Not like they're race cars. Besides, I'll hear the bells ringing."

Gisele shook her head. "I dunno. I think you should reconsider that. Or at least—" She motioned for her brother, who was seated at the window of the bus. "At least get Parker to escort you. I think that makes much better sense."

"Parker?" Valentina said, shaking her head. "Thanks but no thanks. I'd just as soon take my chances on my own."

"What do you have against my brother? Why do you think so badly of him?" Gisele said. "He's a really good guy. He's got wonderful manners. He's kind to others. He gives up his subway seat to old ladies."

Valentina frowned. She didn't want to embroil the man's sister in this at all. But she'd asked; she was forcing her hand in the matter.

"Because long ago your brother humiliated me. He made me feel ashamed and embarrassed and it took forever to live it down and I swore there and then I'd never forgive him. Of course, I never saw him again, so that made it quite easy. But now he's here and the facts are the facts, and I'm sticking to my original plan."

"That's not like Parker to embarrass someone, particularly a girl. What on earth would have prompted him to do that?"

Valentina could feel the rush of shame as if it were yesterday. Her on the beach, pining for him, yearning for the minute when he would bend to her wishes and they'd at last be together. Her stupid, idealistic teen-girl idiocy, front and center for all to laugh at.

"I was in love with your brother," Valentina said. "And when I told him so, he embarrassed me in front of everyone, completely shunning me after inserting the dagger into my heart."

Gisele knit her brow. "Wait a minute. So you're telling me this happened like what, a decade ago? You were maybe fourteen? And he was, let me think," she said, counting backward on her fingers. "So he was maybe twenty? And you told him you loved him and he told you no?"

"You make it sound sort of ridiculous."

"Maybe because that does sound sort of ridiculous," Gisele said. "Parker was a grown man, and you were a young teenager. Just about the same age as his sister at home. The one he worked so hard to protect from guys who wouldn't be so respectful of age differences and vulnerable young women. And so rather than using you and discarding you—like a lot of guys would have happily done, mind you—he politely declined."

"He hardly politely declined," she said. "I barely have to paraphrase it because it's so burned in my brain: 'This,' he said, pointing back and forth between the two of us, 'will never happen, Valentina. I'm a grown-up and you're a child.'"

"But he was speaking honestly. I mean, imagine how awkward it must have been for him—his own sister was the same age. And if some grown-up man propositioned his sister, he'd want to punch the guy. So of course he'd not pursue you. Besides, maybe he was embarrassed that somehow his actions might have led you on."

Valentina paused for a minute as the snow swirled around her. "Look, I really don't want to talk about this anymore. I need to go if I'm going to get my phone before it's ruined. I'll meet you back at the palace."

With that, she took off into a white wall of heavy snowfall.

"Valentina—that's crazy. Don't do that!"

"What's going on?" Parker said, hearing his sister yell at Valentina.

"I told her not to go, but she's chasing the sleigh we were in because her phone is in there and she doesn't want it to be ruined."

Parker shook his head. "You have got to be kidding me. Sometimes I wonder…" But he didn't finish the sentence as he took off after her. With dusk falling, this was no place for her to be wandering in cold and very inclement weather.

It didn't take but a minute for him to catch up to her since the conditions weren't exactly ripe to be able to run on the snow-covered footpaths.

"Are you on some crazy suicide mission or something?" he shouted at Valentina as he reached for her shoulder.

She shrugged him off and continued on, wrapping her arms around herself against the cold.

"Why would you risk running after a stupid phone when you could get lost and hurt out here in the cold and dark? A phone is replaceable, but you're not."

She turned around and glared at him. "Like you care." She knew as soon as she said it that it was the statement of a petulant child.

"Come off it, Valentina," he said. "Of course I care. I'd care if you were the fourteen-year-old-girl with the mean left foot who clobbered all the boys playing soccer. And I'd care if it was the tempestuous but beautiful woman who knows how to leave a man wanting more while working assiduously to ensure that he not get it." He cast a sheepish smile at her.

Valentina kept walking, veering off the path and cutting toward a grove of trees.

Parker stayed right on her heels. "Why do I get the feeling I'm somehow being punished with this crazy scavenger hunt for your missing cell phone?"

"You're the one who insisted on following me," she said. "I was perfectly fine doing this on my own."

"I wouldn't be particularly gentlemanly were I to have let you do this alone. Not that my mother's around to judge me, but I can be sure she'd be deeply disappointed in me if I had."

"So you get your manners from your mother?" she said, winding between trees so heavy with snow that branches were dropping piles of the white stuff on their heads.

"I can't believe we're discussing upbringing while we're being turned into snowmen, but I suppose so," he said. "Considering my father's lack of good grace in the courtesy department, I'd hate to give him credit where credit isn't due."

"Sounds complicated."

"Life's complicated. And currently also quite cold." He rubbed his arms, shivering.

"Look, I just took us on a shortcut that should let us head them off a little ways down here. In fact, I think I see them over there." She pointed toward what looked like a clearing ahead and started running toward it but hit an icy patch. Her legs slipped out from under her, and she went down.

Parker ran toward her, shaking his head. "I'm afraid your cousin Luca failed to mention to me that you are a complete lunatic," he said. "Because why else would you go on this wild-goose chase, risking life and limb? For a phone of all things."

He helped her up, but he saw she was crying. He reached out toward her and wrapped her in his arms. "What's the matter, Valentina? I can't imagine your phone is this important to you."

She nodded. "More important than you can ever imagine."

"But whatever is on there is replaceable."

She shook her head. "Not everything, unfortunately."

He cocked his head and stared at her face. The snow fell now in large chunky flakes, resting on her eyelashes before she could blink them away.

"Is there a photograph on there you're afraid to lose? I'm sure it's backed up somewhere."

"It's not a picture," she said, her voice resigned. "It's the last voice mail I have from my papa before he died. I've held on to this phone for years because I listen to it every night before I go to bed. I need my phone back, and I'm not going to stop until I find it."

Chapter Seventeen

DAMN, women were complicated. Just when he thought he'd figured out that Valentina was a deranged nutter and he should keep very, very far from her, he discovered she was a sentimental fool, willing to risk her own safety to preserve a cherished talisman of her long-lost father.

Parker pondered what he would do if he'd been so lucky as to get one more phone message from his mother before she died, and it brought tears to his eyes.

"Okay, baby, I understand now why this is so very important to you," he said. "But let's think this through. First, I'm going to get hold of Luca and get him to have someone radio the drivers. They can search for your phone and then we can meet up with them somewhere warm and dry to reclaim it." He held her tight as he spoke to her. "Next, I'm going to pull out my phone and figure out on a map exactly where we are and how far from a road, and then I'm going to call an Uber to come get us before we freeze to death. Because I don't know about you, but I'm fairly certain the cousin of the groom dying a gruesome death in the Royal Gardens would pretty much put a damper on the wedding festivities. Am I right?"

He reached his arms out to her shoulders to give her a good, long look.

She frowned and nodded. "I suppose you're right."

"Can I get that in writing?" he said with a wink.

"Don't push your luck. I'm still not exactly speaking to you."

He didn't want to point out that she already *was* speaking to him. No sense in getting her all riled up any more than she already was.

He pulled out his phone and located where they were in the park. "The good news is we're in a city, so eventually you find your way back to civilization," he said. "That said, it might be the difference between frostbite or a cup of hot cocoa. And I'm all for the hot chocolate and not so much for permanent flesh damage. You with me on that?"

She nodded, sniffling.

"So if we turn left and go about five hundred feet, that should put us on a road that borders the park. I'm opening my Uber app so that as soon as we're there, I can summon a ride. All good?"

"But what about my phone?"

His text dinged, and he read the message. "Luca says the driver has the phone and will have it back to the palace probably before we're even there."

She smiled, her large, brown eyes wet from tears.

He reached for her hand. "Hang on to my hand so that you don't fall. We'll be in a warm car in a matter of a few minutes."

They made it to the road and were able to get back to the palace in less than twenty minutes.

"Thanks for the adventure," he said as they sat side by side in the back of the Uber car, trying to warm their icy hands with the heater vent. "Granted, I can think of more interesting ways to spend my time than turning into a human ice cube in a blizzard, but..."

The corner of her mouth lifted in a half smile. "I'm sorry I led you out there like that, Parker. I know it was a fool's errand. I just panicked and didn't know what to do."

"Not a problem," he said. "I would have done the same thing if I were you."

"The thing is, no one knows about this. It's like my own little secret with my father, some special little slice of him I don't have to share with anyone. When he died, it was the thing that helped me through the pain of it, hearing him talk to me every night. I don't know what I'd do if I lost that."

"I'll make a deal with you," he said. "How about we figure out a way to back it up so that you can avoid having to run headlong into a speeding train in order to save it from being crushed on the tracks next time?"

She smiled. "Yeah, I'd like that."

Sure enough, her phone beat her back to the palace, and she smiled, grateful, when it was placed in her palm. The drama of the afternoon had taken it out of Valentina. She just wanted to go hide beneath the blankets of her bed and sleep.

"You sure you don't want to grab some dinner or something?" Parker said, sounding more than hopeful.

She shook her head. "I'm good, thanks. I think I need to just chill. And by chill, I mean warm up. And by warm up, I mean sleep." She didn't want him to think she was suggesting anything. She was tired and confused and had to reconcile the Jerk with the Non-Jerk standing in front of her, and she couldn't do that with him right up in her face.

Once she got to her room, she turned on the gas fireplace and sat on the hearth for a while, just soaking in the heat. Damn, she had to remember to not do something so stupid next time. She was lucky Parker had followed her.

She finally retreated to the warmth of her bed, cocooned in a cloud of soft, downy splendor. As she drifted off to sleep, her mind was a blank slate, which was just fine by her.

It was well after dark when she heard a knock on her door. Valentina pulled up her phone to check the time and saw that it was almost ten o'clock. She'd been asleep for several hours. Good thing she didn't have any wedding commitments this evening, or she'd be in hot water. Though too bad she missed dinner because her stomach was rumbling, and it was probably too late to scrounge up a meal.

She dragged herself up out of the cozy comfort of her bed and walked to the living room, not even bothering to flick on the lights. The view from the floor-to-ceiling windows of her palace apartment revealed the brilliant, twinkling lights of the city decked out in her holiday splendor. She loved Monaforte, there was no two ways about it. This place always rolled out the red carpet for her, showing off her finery to help put a smile on everyone's face.

Valentina peered through the peephole to see Gisele standing outside holding something, so she pulled open the door.

"Girlfriend!" Gisele said, shoving a box of pizza into her hands. "I figured you might be hungry, so I took advantage of the twenty-four-hour food service at this place and ordered up a pizza. Hope you don't mind pepperoni."

Valentina shook her head. "Americans," she said. "You do know pepperoni pizza is decidedly not Italian."

Gisele shrugged. "What can I say? I was a little homesick for New York pizza, so I ordered it up my way."

"I can't even believe they have pepperoni here."

"Knowing this place, some poor under-footman or something had to blanket the mean streets of Porto Castello in search of some cured meat that could adequately pass as American pepperoni." She grinned.

"At least you recognize the error in your ways," Valentina said. "I have to admit I'm partial to pizza bianca myself. When I get down to Rome, I make it a point to visit *Forno Campo de'Fiori* for the best of the best. But I'll attempt your less traditional version since you've gone out of your way to procure it for me."

Gisele laughed. "I've got news for you, pizza elitist. This is about as generic a pizza as they come back home. Besides, it's your only option right now, so here's hoping you like it."

Valentina ushered her inside, looking around in the hallway to ensure there were no others, like, say, Parker, lurking in the shadows. She closed the door and locked it behind her.

"Seriously, Gisele, that was so sweet of you to think of me."

"Yeah, well, you sort of weirded out earlier today, and then when you never materialized at dinner, I got to worrying about you."

"You're kind. But I'm fine. I guess I just needed to catch up on my sleep. But now I'm raring to go," she said, holding up a finger. "Only not so much so that I could be talked into doing shots. Just so you know."

Gisele laughed. "What were we thinking doing those? Seriously bad idea. You should have put a stop to that ASAP."

"Me? You were the one who started!"

"Yeah, but you're the grown-up."

Valentina shook her head. "I thought we established earlier today that you and I are the same age."

"It's true," Gisele said with a nod. "But you were born a few months before me. Which makes you older."

"And wiser, naturally." Valentina winked at her and pulled out two plates from the kitchen, handing one to her friend. "Pizza?" she asked, placing a slice on each plate.

"So if you're so wise, then why do you persist in rejecting Parker?"

Valentina spluttered on a bite of pizza with that unexpectedly blunt question. She poured them both some water and offered a seat in the living room.

"It's like this," Valentina said, crossing her legs. "I realized long ago that your brother was something very abhorrent to me. Like, say, lima beans. Who likes lima beans? Anyone? Not me, I can promise you that. And I've been fine without lima beans all these years. I haven't missed them, not ever.

"So while for ten years I've been convinced that he is one of the worst vegetables known to mankind, now all of a sudden I'm being persuaded that in fact, he is a chocolate milkshake. The problem is I'm so programmed to see him as lima beans, I don't know that I can believe he's actually a chocolate milkshake."

Gisele twirled her finger toward her head, indicating she thought Valentina was crazy.

"Okay, so apologies if I come across as a door-to-door salesman for the Parker Hornsby collection or something. Trust me, I'm not trying to sell you on him or anything. But I do feel the need to defend the man's honor and just have the truth out there. It's only fair."

Valentina nodded. "Your prerogative."

"The thing is, I suspect my brother has as little interest in you as you do in him."

Valentina made a mental eye-roll at that comment because Parker—or at the very least, Parker's man-parts—had made it abundantly clear how he felt about her. Of course, she was just going to pretend her own bits didn't betray her feelings since that would get in the way of the truth.

"Parker has had his share of girlfriends over the years," Gisele said. "Though his main priority since our mother passed away has been me. He was always so worried about making sure I was okay, even if it meant canceling dates. Or not scheduling them at all because he was busy helping me with my homework. Or attending a soccer match I was playing in. Or helping me with my college essays.

"Parker put his life on hold after our mother died, at a

time when he should have been focused on building his own life as a young man, in order to take care of me. Because I was a motherless sixteen-year-old girl who needed a steady influence in my life, and he knew that he was the only one who could provide that for me."

Valentina just stared at Gisele, feeling sort of stupid for many presumptions she might have made about him.

"And then he did start to date, after I was in college. Nobody particularly interesting; none that I'd expect anything too serious of. He was busy with work, and I just don't think relationships were his priority anyhow. But then he started seeing Amanda—who, by the way, I totally hated. Amanda ingratiated herself into our lives very quickly, and soon she was everywhere with us, celebrating holidays and birthdays and practically picking out a china pattern and naming the babies those two would have."

Valentina bristled at the idea that some other woman had even thought about having Parker's babies. Not that she had—of course she'd never think about such a childishly romantic notion as that. Although maybe she did do that a bit when she was fourteen and in love with him.

"And then Parker was at a conference, and he happened upon Amanda and his own business partner going at it in a dark corner of a hotel bar. He couldn't believe it, it was so implausible. Like who does that sort of thing?"

"Evidently Amanda?" Valentina reached for another slice of pizza and handed one to Gisele. "This is pretty good, by the way."

Her friend nodded. "The thing is, Amanda betrayed Parker's trust so severely, I don't know that he's willing or able to commit himself to another woman. It's been too hard for him do that quite yet."

"I'm sorry," Valentina said. "That's really shitty."

"It is. And I'm just telling you this because I think you need to see Parker in a fair light. For years Parker has been my protector. But the truth is, I feel like it's time for me to be his. He's a good man, Valentina. He deserves to be treated as such. And the bottom line is you have nothing to fear in Parker. He's not chasing after you. He doesn't want anything from you. He's just a sweet guy trying to be friendly."

Valentina smiled and nodded, keeping her mouth closed. But she couldn't help but wonder if that was being "just" friendly, what would Parker be like if he was actually putting the moves on her? Which then made her wonder if perhaps she'd love to find out.

Chapter Eighteen

PARKER was beside himself with nerves. Tonight was the pre-wedding gala dinner, tomorrow the wedding, and after that people would be dispersing back to their homes for the holidays. It would be his final chance to make a lasting impression on Valentina, so he knew he had to act. Unfortunately, he had no great tricks up his sleeves, and so far his charm and good looks hadn't gotten him very far. It wasn't like he could just snap his fingers and magically seduce that royal Romeo as much as he'd wish for that to happen.

His sister had decided she'd have more fun getting dressed for the dinner with her new BFF, and the two of them had been gone the whole afternoon, having manis and pedis and blowouts and updos, whatever those were. The very vocabulary of female maintenance was sometimes so confounding.

Truth be told, Parker was fine having the afternoon to himself. He could catch up on some work, tuck away with a book he hadn't touched since the flight to Monaforte, and just enjoy the solitude. He didn't mind dealing with large crowds, but he was also perfectly happy relaxing in the living room, watching the snowfall from the huge picture window. There was, after all, something rather enchanting about being in a historic palace where it felt as if anything could happen (or perhaps already had).

But now it was time to put on the monkey suit and play nice. Tomorrow would be white-tie, but this evening was the less formal black-tie. It didn't take him long to suit up, and once he was ready, his tie straightened six times, his laces tightened against unwanted loosening, he figured he'd sit back with a glass of scotch and wait for the ladies.

Finally at half past six, he knocked on Valentina's door to escort the women. Tonight he was shunning the proffered shuttle bus and instead had hired a limousine to take them to the National Gallery of Art where the dinner would be held.

Parker could hardly believe his eyes when he beheld his kid sister, stunning in an off-the-shoulder satin and silk form-fitting Armani gown in midnight blue. This was his sister who preferred yoga pants and a pair of Asics running shoes to even a pair of blue jeans. He'd never seen her look so grown-up before.

His eyebrows lifted, and he whistled. "Damn, G. You look smokin'. Which is no way for a little sister to be. Now I'm going to have to work twice as hard to keep the men away from you tonight." He reached for his topcoat. "What say you make your brother happy and wear this over your dress tonight?"

She blushed and smacked him playfully on the arm.

"Sorry I'm late," Valentina said, racing into the living room while putting an earring in. She straightened her barely there diamond teardrop necklace, ran her hands down the front of her dress to flatten out any wrinkles, and smiled, looking at Gisele. "So. How do I look?" She held her arms out as if waiting for a dressmaker to pin the dress for alterations.

But then she took one look at Parker's topcoat in his hands and turned five shades of red.

Parker turned and fixed his gaze on Valentina in her champagne-colored sleeveless Monique Lhuillier stretch-satin column gown with a cleavage-hugging surplice neckline. Her hair was smoothed into a chignon, emphasizing her long neck, which only made him want to run his mouth along it. Argh. He felt as if his tongue were glued to the inside of his mouth. Either that or dangling out the side like a lecherous old man.

Finally he collected his thoughts and regained his ability to speak. "You look breathtaking," he whispered, twirling his finger to motion her to turn around so he could see the sexy V-back and train. And a crazy sexy pair of champagne-colored strappy sandals.

Valentina squirmed at the flattery, but Parker wasn't going to let her feel awkward about it. He reached for her hand and pulled it toward his mouth, pressing his lips softly to the back of it.

"*Cara mia*," he said. "*Sei bellissima.*" *You are beautiful.* He'd spent enough time with Luca's family and the Romeos to know plenty of Italian, and only that magical tongue could do her justice at this moment.

"Okay, you two, enough with the gooey stuff," Gisele said. "My stomach is growling. Let's get going so we have plenty of time for hors d'oeuvres."

Valentina nodded, looking relieved that the emphasis was no longer on her. "Let me grab my wrap."

"You're welcome to try this," Parker said, his coat casually dangling from his finger over his shoulder. His eyes burned into hers, willing her to be as turned on as he was. But she only cast her eyes downward. That was okay. He had this. He just knew it deep down in his gut. The only issue was whatever happened to him keeping his distance from Luca's cousin? He was going to have to reconcile that little problem.

They were surprised to see an SUV limousine waiting for them outside.

"With this snow, it was our only option," Laurent, their driver, said.

Valentina, for one, was happy they wouldn't be navigating the snowy streets of Porto Castello in a vehicle ill-equipped for the treacherous road conditions, and they arrived at the National Gallery in a under twenty minutes, which was about nineteen more minutes than she needed to be in a limo with Parker. The sexual tension was so bad you could practically cut it with a knife. It was probably a good thing Parker's sister was there or she'd likely have pounced on him like a cat on a mouse.

She felt much safer once they arrived at the gallery and she could mingle amongst the hundreds of guests and not feel the laser-sharp focus of Parker's attention homed in on her. Although as the cocktail hour progressed, she could still sense his presence; no matter where she stood, he was there.

And of course, as Luca and Larkin has assured her that first night, he was again seated next to her for dinner. She couldn't decide if she was thrilled or terrified to have him in in her thrall. On the one hand, it was flattering that he was so fixed on her. But on the other, it made her feel such responsibility. To do what, she wasn't sure. She wasn't even clear if she could or would choose to act on his entreaties. In fact, she had no freaking idea what to do. Her body was yelling at her to do one thing, but her brain was putting on the brakes, and her brain was probably the one she should listen to.

These formal dinners meant a very complicated—not to mention historical—table: every place setting was measured to within the eighth of an inch. Each of the two hundred guests had ten pieces of silver-gilt cutlery at their place as well as six crystal glasses: for water, champagne, white wine, red wine, sweet wine, and port. Each guest had his or her own butter dish with two pats of butter stamped with the royal crown—yes, even the butter was personalized. Huge floral arrangements in gilded vases atop buffed mirrored trays were placed every five feet along the tables. Between the flowers were four-foot-tall candelabras that had belonged to the royal family since the seventeenth century. The porcelain dishes were more than two hundred years old.

Negotiating a meal at such a formal table could be tricky if you were unfamiliar with the etiquette. Valentina had attended many over the years and was well aware of how to manage. She felt a little bad that she hadn't thought to coach Gisele on the ins and outs of dining at a royal dinner, and she was curious to see how Parker would do.

But true to form, he handled each course like a pro. And he conversed with the seatmate on his other side almost as if Valentina wasn't even there. Which made her feel a bit jealous. But just as the third course of salmon was delivered, she felt his left hand come to rest atop her thigh. She was fairly certain that didn't meet with royal dining protocol, but… It felt warm and appropriate right there, with him possessively stroking her leg with his thumb. He continued to chat with the woman to his right as Valentina talked to the minister of something or other who was seated to her left. As necessary throughout the course of the evening, Parker would remove his hand so that he could cut his meat or whatever was being served. But then he would discreetly slip it right back afterward. Occasionally they'd exchange casual conversation.

"The roast is delicious," he would say with a wink, and she would try to figure out if there was some double entendre there.

"I've been dying for something sweet," she said as dessert was finally served. "You?"

"I was thinking something wet would be even more refreshing."

And Valentina's eyes grew wide, because there was no mistaking what he meant by that.

She choked as she took a large sip of her after-dinner wine, which was far sweeter than she wanted.

"Um, yes," she said, unable to come up with anything else.

"What about you, Valentina? Something a little firmer perhaps?"

She glanced to her left and his right, hoping like hell no one had heard him say those things to her.

"I understand the after-dinner liqueurs will be taken in another room," she said. "Perhaps then I can give you a little tour of more *private parts* of the gallery."

It was Parker's turn to choke. "I'd like that," he said after clearing his throat. "Shall I bring my topcoat?"

She shook her head. "I think we'll have plenty of body heat without it."

So much for not knowing what to do about Parker Hornsby.

Chapter Nineteen

PARKER could not wait to unload his snifter of brandy and watched closely to see when Valentina began to migrate away from the room. He gave it a minute, set his glass down, then followed in that direction. His sister was engrossed in intense conversation with Tomasso Romeo, so he had the presence of mind to shoot her a quick text.

"If you can't find me when you're ready to leave, just catch a ride back with Tomasso," he wrote.

"You up to no good?" she texted back.

"With any luck."

"Don't do anything I wouldn't do."

"That is so not the thing to say to your brother. I never want you to do anything that I might do. Ever. Even if it's clean and legal and aboveboard."

"Okay then, have fun with Valentina!" She added a few heart emojis for emphasis. Ugh.

"I never said I was going to be with Valentina."

"I wasn't born yesterday, Parker."

Parker turned his phone to silent and slipped off down a corridor marked DO NOT ENTER, hoping like hell Valentina wasn't playing a trick on him and ready to have him sent to the gallows for crimes against the state.

After turning down one corridor and then another, he came upon Valentina standing before a very large portrait—some five feet high and a good eleven feet long—of a naked man and woman entwined in half recline on a sumptuous and elaborately carved bed, a decrepit elderly woman spying on them behind a cracked door while hushing her little dog.

"*Two Lovers*," she said. "By Giulio Romano. Painted in the sixteenth century. The work is on loan from the Hermitage in Saint Petersburg. Romano is said to have apprenticed with Raphael in Rome, and he took over Raphael's workshop upon his death. Romano famously fled Rome for Mantua for fear of persecution from the Catholic Church over a book in which he illustrated a series of images depicting sexual positions. Eventually it became a bestseller in Europe, which goes to show yet again that there's no such thing as bad publicity."

Parker raised an eyebrow. "Racy fellow, this Romano."

"What can I say? He's Italian of course."

"And Italians make better lovers?"

"You'll have to decide that for yourself," she said, her eyes twinkling. "*Two Lovers*, which some say features Zeus, others Ares, was a commissioned work that disappeared for a few hundred years until it showed up at the Hermitage. Even then still considered indecent, it wasn't until about a hundred years ago that it was included in gallery catalogs."

"Shame for something so beautiful—and erotic—to be kept out of reach."

"Maybe makes it all the better when it becomes available."

"I can see how it might have been considered salacious back then," he said with an approving grin that let her know he found it to be perfectly entertaining. "Particularly considering where her hand is." He rubbed his chin with his thumb and forefinger. "Kind of reminds me of something."

Valentina blushed. The woman in the portrait's hand was sliding beneath a sheet that barely covered the man's penis. Awfully familiar to the two of them, all things considered.

"And you brought me here to show me this because?"

She shook her head. "No particular reason," she said. "I thought you might find it interesting. It's part of a show of erotic art from the Renaissance. I'm particularly partial to Renaissance art I suppose, given my family's history and patronage of the arts for many hundreds of years."

"Yes, but are you partial to erotic art?"

She smiled a tiny, mysterious smile. "It seems to be growing on me."

"Well, I've just discovered that I am," he said. "Who knew?" He shrugged, lifting his arms up. "And now, as if I hadn't already wanted you like crazy, I'm dying to see if we can recreate that very pose."

She arched an eyebrow. "So instead of dressing in costumes for role-playing, you think we should reenact famous portraits of lovers caught in the act?"

He grabbed her hand. "For now, why don't we find somewhere nearby that doesn't have security cameras focused on it? Please. Or else we'll be very caught in the act. And to be honest, I'd rather create our own positions if that's all the same to you."

Valentina quickly pulled him down another hallway and into a room with an old-fashioned-looking velvet sofa and several mirrors along the walls with individual chairs tucked beneath a counter facing the mirrors.

"It's a sitting room off a women's bathroom," she said. "Back in the day, women would relax in here and freshen their makeup, perhaps rest on the sofa, enjoy a cigarette away from the prying eyes of men who didn't approve of women smoking."

"So a very private room then," he said, leading her toward the sofa.

"Very." She pushed him onto the couch as she fell down next to him.

"God, I've been dying to do this." He pulled her toward him, pressing his mouth to hers as he wrapped his arms around her. For minutes it seemed they were in silence but for the sound of their breathing and the occasional sigh one or the other would heave. Parker reached for the hem of Valentina's dress and shifted the material up until it encircled her waist.

"I hope this doesn't wrinkle, or everyone's going to know what I've been up to."

"We'll figure it out," he said as he pulled her on top of him, her very wet center pressed against his swollen cock, still contained inside his tuxedo pants. He pulled Valentina down with one hand, giving him access to her mouth while using his other hand to slide through her slick center, rubbing and swirling his fingers on her swollen clit as she moved against him faster and faster.

"Parker, this isn't enough," she said, shifting away and quickly unbuttoning his pants, sliding them down. "Please tell me you came prepared."

He grabbed for his wallet.

"Fool me once, shame on me…," he said as he pulled a condom from the wallet and tore the packet open in record time. "Trust me, never again will I allow myself to be caught with my pants down, as it were."

"Oh I don't mind the pants down. Just as long as I can act on that." She smiled a devilish grin.

He sheathed himself quickly and pulled Valentina on top of him again, and she ever so slowly lowered herself onto his cock until he was balls-deep. He groaned as Valentina ground herself on him, pressing and shifting in a circular motion as she lifted and then lowered again. Parker closed his eyes to the pleasure while fumbling with his fingers to slip beneath the bodice of her evening gown. He pinched her nipples, and she moaned loudly.

He pulled her closer, allowing him to nuzzle his mouth toward a breast, and soon his teeth found a nipple and he bit down hard, prompting Valentina to increase the pace of her hips rising and falling on his cock.

"That's it, Valentina," he said. "I feel it. Do you? Are you close?"

She replied by pumping harder, and he pressed his fingers to her center, crazily turned on as he felt his cock disappearing into her body.

"I can't hold it anymore. Come with me, baby. Now." Parker groaned loudly as he froze, urging himself deep into Valentina just as she called out his name and pressed hard on him. He could feel her muscles ripple around him, milking his climax till he thought he couldn't take it

anymore, the feeling was so unbelievable.

Parker lay there, unable to move but feeling as relaxed and happy as he had in a long, long time.

Talk about the perfect climax to his day.

Chapter Twenty

OF course Valentina felt conflicted. She'd just had incredible sex with the handsomest man in the place. And had she mentioned that it was incredible? Something about him brought out some unrequited horniness she didn't quite know what to do with. Which meant she'd love to take him back to her apartment at the palace so they could fuck like rabbits till dawn. But (*a*) she couldn't stay up all night when tomorrow was the wedding since she desperately needed a good night's sleep, and (*b*) no way could she allow anyone to see him sneaking in or out of her apartment, 'cause she'd never live that down.

Plus what would they do about Gisele? She'd notice him missing of course. And the first thing she'd do would be to come to Valentina and say she needed help finding her brother. Who of course would be naked and possibly even tied to the bed if Valentina had her way, and then what would she say to Gisele?

After she and Parker lay there for some time recouping their lost energy stores, she rallied them.

"We've got to slip out before the party ends or there will be problems," she said as she stood and pulled her dress down, trying hard to press out the wrinkles in her gown but having little success. It didn't help matters that her hair was a shambles and her lipstick smeared on her mouth. Oy, what was she going to do?

Parker was zipping and buttoning relevant articles of clothing and pulling his cummerbund back into position when Valentina looked at his crotch.

"Oh, Parker," she said, pointing at it. "I'm so sorry." There was a visible wet spot where Valentina had rubbed herself against him earlier.

"I think you'll need to follow closely behind me so that no one notices," she said. "And in the meantime, hopefully they won't figure out that I look like I just had a quickie in the ladies' room."

"But you did just have a quickie in the ladies' room."

"Correction: ladies' lounge."

"Point taken," he said. As they walked by *the Two Lovers*, Parker gave the couple a quick thumbs-up.

"Thanks, Zeus," he said with a grin as Valentina playfully smacked his bottom to get him moving.

"Zeus has nothing to do with your good fortune," she said. "That's all me."

"Believe me, I'll be thanking you for days to come."

As they returned to the main gallery, crowds were beginning to thin out, so they got Parker's coat and her wrap and called for their driver, allowing them to slip out unnoticed.

They feigned indifference to one another once back at the palace, just in case someone might notice them together. When they reached their apartments, Valentina reverted to business-as-usual Valentina instead of just-enjoyed-intimate-sex-with-the-man Valentina.

"Okay, so, well, good night then," she said. "Thanks for a fun night."

"Oh, no you don't," Parker said, slipping a foot between the door and the doorjamb. "I knew you would try to pretend nothing happened again."

"Parker," Valentina said with a sigh. "We've got a big day tomorrow. We need a good night's sleep."

"I know," he said. "And what better way to sleep like a baby than a little tumble between the sheets followed by a cozy spooning of our bodies?"

He heard voices down the hall and quickly pulled her toward him and pressed them both inside the doorway, shutting the door quietly.

"My sister," he said. "And some guy. He better just be acting the gentleman and walking her back to her room. But to be honest, I really don't want to deal with whatever that is. Looks like you're stuck with me. I promise I won't keep you awake. Not any longer than you'd like to be."

"Parker Hornsby, you are going to be the death of me," she said. But he pulled her toward him and placed his mouth over hers, and managed to put an official end to any and all objections she might have thought about raising.

There was no cock crowing at dawn, though there was a certain someone's cock that maybe wanted to crow, but Valentina needed to get rid of Parker before anyone detected they'd been together, so she practically pushed him out of bed and sent him on his way.

"Can we spend time together later?"

"No," Valentina said as she ushered him toward the door. "It's bad luck to see the bridesmaid before the wedding."

"Isn't that the bride, and it applies to the groom only?"

She shook her head. "I'm making this up as I go along. Humor me."

He reached for her to get one last kiss before he got to the door. "Now, no going all cold-shoulder on me later, right?"

"Go, go," she said, managing to not respond to that ten-million-dollar question. Because she really couldn't make promises she couldn't keep.

Chapter Twenty-One

JUST as Parker slipped from apartment thirteen, he heard a noise and looked to see a shadowy figure backing away from apartment eleven where, theoretically, his sister was fast asleep.

"Stop!" he said in a loud whisper.

"Ack!" said the person, who turned out to be none other than Valentina's brother Tomasso.

"What are you doing leaving my sister's apartment at this hour?" Parker hoped Tomasso wouldn't turn that question right around on him, hoping instead that Tomasso didn't even know his sister was staying there.

"Parker! Fancy meeting you here. You're"—he pointed from the door Parker had just left to Parker and back again—"just leaving as well, I see?"

But Parker wasn't having any of it. "Where's Gisele? What are you doing here?"

Tomasso held up his hands. "It's all good, my friend. Your sister and I got to talking and it was late, so I just fell asleep on the sofa. I guess she went to bed because I didn't see her. I wanted to get back to my own bed to catch a few hours of sleep before the wedding."

Parker eyed him suspiciously. "Okay then, you should get going."

Tomasso ran his fingers through his thick, wavy dark hair. Parker cursed those Italian men who looked as good at dawn after sleeping on a couch as they did the night before in a fresh tuxedo. Come to think of it, the two of them here in their rumpled formal wear didn't bode well, did it?

Tomasso took the cue and practically ran down the hall, leaving Parker to return to his apartment and hopefully catch a few hours of sleep.

"Well, well, well, look what the cat dragged in," Gisele said when Parker came into the living room around noon.

Parker yawned, stretched, and rubbed his belly. "Speaking of tomcats," he said. "Does the name Tomasso ring any bells?"

Gisele blushed. "What?"

"A certain Italian stallion was seen leaving this apartment somewhere around dawn. Any idea why?"

"And who might have seen him leaving? Maybe someone who was trying to sneak back into said apartment?" She crossed her arms and drummed her fingers.

"Let's not worry about me," he said. "I'm a grown-up."

"Um, news flash, sweetie," his sister said. "Me too. Besides, if you're going to play the 'who's the grown-up card,' Valentina and I are the same age, so what goes for one goes for the other."

Parker pursed his lips. "Tomasso said you two were just talking. Let's hope that's all it was."

Gisele glanced at her watch. "Gee, look at the time. We need to start getting ready!" With that, she scurried out of the living room and into her bedroom.

"We're not done with this conversation, you know," Parker said.

"Just as soon as you're ready to talk to me about you and Valentina, then we can discuss me!"

Women. Parker rolled his eyes and poured a cup of coffee for reinforcement. It was going to be a long day.

Once again, the women chose to get ready together, leaving Parker on his own. At half past four, he stood at the base of the Grande Staircase, drumming his fingers against his crossed arms, impatient for Gisele and Valentina to arrive. They needed to be at the church no later than five for the seven-o'clock candlelight service, and he was determined to make sure they were on time.

He kept glancing at the top of the steps. When finally he caught his first glimpse of Valentina, his breath hitched in his chest.

She stood at the top of the wide, red-carpeted staircase, absolutely enchanting in an embroidered royal-blue silk crepe gown with an overlay of chiffon softening the overall effect and causing her to look positively royal.

The bodice and sleeves were a lace illusion. Draped across her shoulders was a coordinating cape with a small train that accented the gown's train.

She wore long, elegant white gloves, a silver velvet sash—from the order of the royal cherubim—secured with a diamond-encrusted bee pin, the symbol of the Romeos since the time of the Renaissance. Her hair was scraped back loosely in a chignon with loose tendrils framing her face, and atop her head was a diamond-and-sapphire tiara that sparkled when it caught the light, even more so because some of the gems were set *en tremblant*, so they moved with the wearer.

Until now, Parker hadn't given true thought to the royal lineage from which Valentina hailed. But she was indeed a princess in all but official title, standing atop the staircase as if she owned this palace.

He wiped a tear from the corner of his eye, feeling a little wimpy for getting all worked up just looking at her. But how could he not? She was so breathtaking.

When she arrived at the bottom of the steps, he reached for her hand.

"I thought you were supposed to let the bride shine on her big day."

"I will."

He sized her up from her dazzling tiara to her custom-dyed satin Manolo Blahnik pumps. "I'm sure that was your intent," he said. "But I'm afraid you will be, hands down, the most beautiful woman in that cathedral."

She blushed and smiled. "Why thank you, Parker. You're none too shabby yourself in your handsome white-tie ensemble. You look positively edible." She licked her lips and he groaned.

"I'll be counting the minutes till dessert then," he said with a wolfish grin, locking elbows as he escorted her to their limo.

Chapter Twenty-Two

PEOPLE were filing into the Cathedral of *Santo Giacomo il Maggiore* in droves. For royal weddings like this, guests ran the gamut from other royals throughout the world to heads of state to family members. The glow of thousands of candles warmed the chilly cathedral as guests streamed in through the massive wooden doors of the towering medieval Gothic cathedral.

Valentina peered from the holding area where they were waiting to watch the processional of guests taking their seats. There were many men in military uniforms, replete with badges and medals plastered all over their dress coats. Others had dressed in national costumes, and many, like Valentina, looked positively royal in sashes and badges and tiaras.

Valentina seemed only to have eyes for Parker in his formal wing-collared white shirt and tie topped with a Marcella waistcoat and a black tailcoat with silk lapels. He looked from another era, so formal and elegant. And gorgeous. No wonder she fell so madly for him back when she was young. What wasn't to love? Except, well, when she didn't love him so much. But still. Sometimes things changed, and she didn't want to be seen as not being willing to reevaluate decisions along the way.

Before the actual ceremony began, the wedding attendants marched two by two down the nave, or center aisle, of the church. Little did anyone know, it was the first official "outing" for Parker and Valentina, linked as they were, arm in arm. Valentina let out a tiny wave as she passed her mother and brothers and then her aunt, the queen, and her uncle. She wondered if they could read on her face how she was feeling. As they approached the altar, they turned to take seats opposite the choir and kept their fingers locked as they remained seated side by side.

Luca stepped from the shadow, taking his place at the altar to await his bride. He looked sharp in his navy-blue tailcoat with brass buttons, corded wrists, badges, and stars and bars with colors and shoulder rank boards. He looked as if he alone could command a fleet of sailors or a platoon of soldiers.

A trumpet voluntary began to swell from the organ, and all eyes turned toward the back to see Larkin, resplendent in a hand-embroidered ivory satin gown with thousands of pearls sewn into the heart-shaped bodice. She wore a Basque-lace veil that draped over her face, trailing atop a fifty-foot train that was held aloft by a cadre of adorable children in coordinating ivory taffeta gowns as their white patent leather shoes clicked quietly on the stone floor.

The archbishop welcomed the guests to the nuptials of Prince Luca and Larkin, and the long service began. Throughout the service, Parker and Valentina exchanged glances and smiles, and when Luca and Larkin exchanged vows, the two attendants squeezed their fingers together.

Church bells pealed as the couple was officially pronounced man and wife, and Luca and his princess kissed, then turned toward their adoring audience and, hands clasped, held their arms aloft to a great cheer from the crowd. They proceeded down the nave to the awaiting horse-drawn carriage that would take them back to the palace. Despite the winter chill and the continued snowfall, the parade route to the palace would be lined with well-wishers from throughout the country.

Each pair of wedding attendants rode in their own smaller covered carriages, which protected them from the weather, and as luck would have it, prying eyes.

Because once Parker had made certain Valentina was secure in the carriage and their footman had closed the door behind them, he leaned into her and swiped his tongue to her lips, urging a kiss from her mouth.

She complied, her warm mouth settling over his as their tongues entwined.

Valentina pulled away and laughed. "You know, your sister, when she was pretending to not try to sell me on you, told me that your kissing me all those years ago would have been like kissing your sister. What do you have to say to that?"

Parker mulled over that for a minute. "Wellllll...," he said, pushing her cape out of the way to clear a path for him to kiss her neck. "I never like to think of my sister when I'm in the middle of trying to kiss the woman I think I love—"

"Wait a minute—did you just say the woman you think you love?"

"Aha... I though perhaps you'd miss that comment."

"Nothing gets by me," she said. "Especially the man I think I always knew I loved."

"Does that mean what I think it means?"

"Yes but I want you to finish answering my question."

"Back then, of course it would have been when you were still a child. So of course I'd never have entertained the idea of kissing you at that age. It *would* have been like kissing my sister."

He winked at her, then continued to kiss his way along her throat and back up to her mouth. "But trust me, the grown woman before me is nothing like my sister," he said, his lips paving a warm and tingly trail over her flesh. "Thank God for that."

"Because you would never want to kiss your sister?"

"Because I never want to stop kissing you," he said. "And if I have any say in these matters, you and I will be busy getting reacquainted for a good long while."

"Is that a promise or a threat?"

"Both," he said, pulling her closer to him. "Because I'm never going to risk losing you again. I've got to make up for a lot of lost time. Do we have a deal?"

Valentina nodded, linking her fingers with his. "Sealed with a kiss then?"

"Indeed." He locked them both in a passionate kiss to indeed seal the deal.

Thank you so much for reading *Red Carpet Romeo!* I hope you enjoyed it! If so, please help others find this book:

1. Help other people find this book by writing a review.

2. Sign up for my new releases email so you can find out about the next book as soon as it's available and get fun giveaways.
   http://eepurl.com/baaewn

3. Like my Facebook page.
   www.facebook.com/jennygardinerbooks

And I love to hear from readers! Let me know what you think about my books! You can write to me at jenny@jennygardiner.net, and visit me on the web at www.jennygardiner.net.

Turn the page for a sneak peek of the next book in The Royal Romeos – **Blue Collar Romeo**!

Blue Collar Romeo

Chapter One

GISELE Hornsby kept pinching herself, even as she brushed on a third application of mascara, hoping a bit more make-up might distract from her bloodshot, hung-over eyes. She still couldn't believe she was here, in Monaforte, a guest for a romantic royal wedding, the plus-one of her brother Parker for the event of the season. It was enough to make even the most hung-over of girls swoon.

She'd arrived in the fairytale country of Monaforte, a small European principality nestled between Italy and Switzerland, with her brother—college friends with the groom, Prince Luca—earlier in the week, in time for the many pre-nuptial events that were scheduled to take place. They even got to stay as royal guests in an apartment in the palace. Where all the royal people lived! Life could not get any cooler.

Gisele had spent her first full day touring Porto Castello, the charming and historic capital of Monaforte, with her new friend Valentina Romeo, a royal cousin of Luca's, and for some as yet undisclosed reason, her brother's adversary. Gisele was determined to get to the bottom of the mystery as to why Valentina threw daggers at Parker whenever he looked her way, and why her normally chill brother had turned suddenly surly.

She mistakenly thought tequila would unlock the answer, and proceeded to get both Valentina and herself sloppy drunk in the middle of the afternoon at a quaint little seaside pub, though never did get to the root of the problem before Valentina's super hot brother Tomasso stopped them before they made complete fools of themselves in public.

He was at an advantage, what with his jaw-dropping good looks—he was tall, with wavy, dark hair, the most expressive amber eyes, broad shoulders and chest, and a truly perfect tight butt tucked into a sexy pair of jeans. What self-respecting girl who hadn't been laid in a long while wouldn't capitulate to the guy? So despite the two women having far too much fun for a weekday afternoon, they relented, paid up the bar bill, and returned to the palace at his insistence, whereupon Gisele promptly passed out for a few hours before the next royal bash was to start.

Her alarm went off with just enough time to get ready for the party, to be held at the country home of Luca's brother and heir apparent to the throne, Prince Adrian and his wife Emma. As soon as the phone blared its reveille, she made a mental note to switch her alarm from the pre-programmed "marimba" tone to something with a little less sensory overload for her throbbing brain next time. Even though she wasn't going to have a next time, since she'd also made a mental note to remember that tequila wasn't the answer and only led to pain and suffering after the fun wore off. For that very reason, she popped a couple of Advil to tamp down the headache that was threatening to ruin her evening, slapped on some face paint, and hoped no one would be the wiser to her flagging state of mind.

After slinking into a tea-length strapless cocktail dress with a silver beaded bodice and soft black tulle skirt, she twisted her long, blond waves into a soft side-braid, then slid on a pair of black Stuart Weitzman strappy sandals with heels that made her legs look gorgeous. She turned to the side in front of the mirror, smoothing down her gown at her waistline, then applied a coat of dark pink lipstick, fluttered her lashes over her bright blue eyes, pressed her lips together and nodded to herself.

"Perfect," she said. "No one will be the wiser that I feel like complete crap."

She grabbed her jacket from the closet and stepped into the living room to join Parker, who stood by the door, coat already on and buttoned up, arms crossed, eyes fixed on his watch, tapping his toe impatiently.

"What?" Gisele said, grinning. "I'm like thirty seconds late."

Parker threw her the side-eye. "Thirty seconds give or take five minutes. Besides, if you hadn't invoked my good name in conversation with your equally drunk friend this afternoon, just think, you could have actually been early. Now we'll probably not even get a seat on the bus." The palace was providing transportation to all of the guests to Luca's country estate.

Gisele rolled her eyes. "I love you, Parks, but you can be a little fastidious sometimes. Relax, sweet brother," she said. "It's all good. There will definitely be a seat on the bus. Plus, I didn't make anything worse for you, and besides, I got to meet Valentina's cute brother. I'd say it's a win-win."

He shook his head. "You were never good at keeping score, G," he said, reaching for her hand and pulling her out the door. "Your sticking your nose into my business means I lose. Now, come on, or I'm going to get stuck sitting on that Valentina woman's lap and at this rate, lord knows what sort of torture she'd impose on me then."

Parker didn't exactly have to sit on Valentina's lap, but did in fact have to tuck into the next row up from her, the only seats left on the bus thanks to Gisele's timing. After a little shuffling at the behest of the girls, Gisele wedged in next to Valentina, which meant Parker got to sit next to Tomasso. Gisele threw a hard glare at her brother.

"What?" he said, squinting his eyes at her.

She knit her brows and nudged her head in the direction of his seatmate, trying to convey that she wanted to sit next to Tomasso. But her dense brother just frowned, his lips pursed solemnly to send her a silent message to leave him the hell alone.

Grrrr. Can't a girl get a little one-on-one time in a dark bus with a gorgeous Italian man? She was going to have to work on that one a bit.

Gisele's eyes opened wide in amazement as the bus approached the estate, which was surrounded by a tall brick wall, draped with holly and pine roping entwined with white lights for the holiday season. The bus passed a large, brick guardhouse flanked by stone-faced men with bright red uniforms and tall furry hats—what was with royals and those hats?—then continued along a tree-lined driveway for a mile or so before finally stopping in the pebbled parking area of the palatial Georgian country estate.

As they lined up to get off the bus, Gisele couldn't help but press up gently against Tomasso. After all, people were clamoring to get out, there was no room to move. That was her excuse, anyhow, and she enjoyed feeling his solid body pressed to hers in the dark. At least it let her fantasize for a minute what it would be like to be pressed up horizontally with the man, rather than vertical, as she waited to step down from the damned bus.

They followed in a line up the slate walkway, entering through two oversized doors hung with giant Christmas wreaths. As two butlers greeted guests and collected coats, Gisele tried to stick close to Parker so she wouldn't feel too out of place, but he no sooner handed off his coat than he disappeared, leaving her standing by the doorway knowing not a soul.

"I'd offer you a drink, but that's probably the last thing you want right about now," she heard a deep voice from behind say.

She turned to see Tomasso, stylish in a dark blue Ermenegildo Zegna suit she recognized as similar to one her brother had tried on when they went shopping for the wedding. God, she loved a man in a well-fitted, sexy Italian suit.

She rolled her eyes. "I'm not sure if I should reprimand you for spoiling our good fun or thank you for it," she said, rubbing her temples against the throb of the headache that even the ibuprofen didn't seem to touch. "But, I think my only choice tonight is to double down against that evil tequila. Maybe temper it with some more genteel champagne?"

Tomasso reached for two glasses of champagne from a passing waiter and handed her a flute.

"In that case, here's to the hair of the dog," he said, clinking glasses with her.

"Ugh. I prefer my dogs to be of the four-legged variety, thanks," she said. "Not the kind that somehow mysteriously penetrate your brain and bark and scratch to get out while you feel as if your eyeballs are going to pop right out of their sockets."

"You make drinking shots sounds so pleasant."

"Shots are never pleasant after the fact. It's only while you're in the middle of doing them they seem like such a great idea."

"You could say the same thing about relationships," he said with a grimace.

She lifted an eyebrow. "Well, if that's not the most cynical comment du jour, especially considering you're here for a romantic wedding."

He rolled his eyes. "You don't buy into that happily ever after nonsense, do you?" he said. "These things are little more than mergers. Sort of like two businesses that think they can work together but when it comes down to it, one of the two ends up suffering for it."

Gisele shook her hand as if she'd just touched something hot. "Wow," she said. "I'm surprised you even bothered to show for this. Why on earth are you celebrating something you clearly don't see worthy of any such joy?"

He shrugged. "Let's see…Because my mother made me?" he said. "Besides, it's more like a family reunion, and who doesn't like a family reunion?"

Gisele pursed her lips. She and Parker had never had

the chance to indulge in things like family get-togethers, what with their very broken family.

"I wouldn't know," she said, throwing back a gulp of champagne.

"Thirsty?" he said, cocking his eyebrow and grinning.

"I'd just rather tamp down my hangover with good champagne than have attention drawn to the fact that I don't really have a family with whom I could commune."

"Homeless, are you?"

"More like orphaned."

He scrunched his nose. "I'm sorry," he said. "I was only joking. Didn't mean to poke fun at you."

"Poke away," she said. "Families come in all shapes and sizes. Mine just happens to be minuscule and be made up of me and my brother Parker."

"Well Parker practically seems like family to us," he said. "After spending so many holidays with him I feel like he's my brother from another mother."

She shrugged. "Great for Parker. Where does that leave me?"

"I'm sure we can throw you in as honorary family member," he said. "You'll be the two-fer."

"Gee, that's flattering," she said. "Sort of like, 'well, we don't know you, and we have no reason to do this but maybe a hint of pity, but sure, why don't you pretend you're one of us just for the hell of it.'"

"Now who's the cynic?" He winked at her.

"I guess we're a great pair, aren't we?"

"So when you're not protecting your sister's honor, what do you do?"

"By that do you mean what do I do, or what do I want to do?"

She toed the ground with the front of her sandals. "I didn't know I was asking such a loaded question. I don't know; humor me. How about what do you want to do?"

"I don't know what you know about my family—"

"Well we're practically related, so obviously I'm completely in the know." She grinned.

"Yeah, that. So in that case you know that my brothers and sister and I are carrying on the tradition of Romeos from as far back as the Middle Ages in producing fine Italian wines. And because of that tradition, there is an expectation that all Romeos must follow in these footsteps and help to run the family business."

"But you are like that elf who wanted to be a dentist instead of making toys."

Tomasso knit his brows. "Huh?"

"You know, from Rudolph the Red-Nosed Reindeer, that Christmas special. The song," she held out her hands to prepare him for it, then started singing, "Why am I such a misfit?"

"Okay…"

She placed her hand on his shoulder. "No, really. Clearly you missed the show so I'll give you the brief run-down. Rudolph has a red nose, which means he's an outcast. He meets Hermey, an elf who hates making toys and wants to be a dentist. They set off on an epic adventure, yada yada, and they all live happily ever after once they tame the Abominable Snow Monster."

One side of Tomasso's mouth curved up into a grin. "There goes that happily ever after nonsense again."

"Of course. You can't have a Christmas special without a happy ending," she said. "So did you want to be a dentist, then?" She burst out laughing at her own joke.

"Um, no," he said. "Should I?"

"I'm so sorry," she said, shaking her head. "Sometimes Parker gets really mad at me that I have no filter. Which means I can be the life of the party but sometimes I just blather on a bit longer than I should. So go ahead, you tell me what it is that you want to do."

Tomasso glanced to either side. "I'm wondering if there is someplace we can sit down because at this rate this is going to be till midnight until I actually get a chance to speak."

Gisele frowned. "Seriously, I'll shut up," she said, pretending to zip her mouth shut and swallowing the key, then reconsidering the gesture. "You know that never made much sense to me, swallowing the key, because your mouth is already zipped shut, right? So how would you open it to swallow the key? And then once it's swallowed, how can you ever open it again?"

Tomasso grabbed two more flutes of champagne as another tray passed them by.

"As I was saying," he said, dipping his head and looking at her like he thought she was nuts. "I'd rather be working with my hands. I realized I'm quite a gifted woodworker, and I like it. Whereas before, I sort of hated every day I was stuck living this proscribed life over which I had no true control. Don't get me wrong, I have a great life. And I'm fortunate for my ancestors who built up this successful business as they have. And it's not that I don't like wine; I love it. I'm just sort of bored and looking for something that ignites a fire in me."

Gisele eyed him from head to toe. Speaking of igniting a fire... This man was awfully easy on the eyes. And he seemed like he had a heart—at least to the extent that he wanted to honor his own wishes and desires and not simply capitulate to expectations.

"Wow," she said. "I really respect you for that. Oh, wait—" She pretended to unzip her mouth and pull out the key. "Sorry, that was a joke Parker and I shared when we were kids. I am so in the habit of doing that. Okay, so my mouth is unlocked now, I can go on. As I was saying, good for you, doing what speaks to your soul. You only get one life; you've got to live it the way you want to."

He nodded. "I'm glad you understand," he said. "Because the rest of my family doesn't seem to grasp it so much."

"Yeah, well, now that I'm honorary family and all, just leave it to me to smooth over the ruffled feathers."

He laughed. "They'll get over it," he said. "I know my mamma already understands. I worked so hard when we built our new corporate headquarters, and finally she could see the fruits of my labor."

"So tell me about this," she said, placing her hand on his. "I'd like to hear all about it."

He reached for her elbow and guided her toward an alcove with a small love seat, then motioned for her to sit down, then he took the spot next to her.

"I want to be sure I'm not boring you too much," he said with a small laugh. "This way if you start to nod off, you won't have far to fall."

Gisele waved her hand at him dismissively. "Nonsense. I can't wait to hear about it."

"So my eldest brother Sandro, who really became our surrogate father after our papà passed, had ambitious plans to build a grand headquarters for Cantine dei Marchesi Romeo wines, one that would attract tourists, a destination venue. As the plans progressed it became even more grandiose, and the final outcome was a collaboration with the premier architects and building specialists the world-over who helped to create this gorgeous building. It's environmentally friendly, designed to blend in harmony with the landscape. Whenever possible, we used natural resources in the building and decorating of it. It's really a work of art in the Tuscan countryside, and the inside, mamma mia, it's breathtaking."

Gisele had leaned forward to listen more closely. She could barely concentrate on his words, transfixed as she was with his looks, not to mention the feel of his hard legs practically pressed up next to hers. This man was so interesting, and so, well, sensual, the way his hands moved as he spoke, as if he was speaking a whole different language with them. She tried to picture those strong, rough hands roaming her body and found herself stifling a moan.

"I'd love to see your contributions to the project," she said.

"Really?" he said. "I've got my laptop back at the palace. Maybe I can bring it over to your apartment and show you some images."

Gisele arched her brow. If this was anything like him bringing his "etchings" to show her... she was totally on board. And maybe she could show him some of her own "etchings"... After all, it had been far too long since she'd been up close and personal with a man.

She reached into her small clutch and found a small breath mint, which she discreetly slipped into her mouth.

"I'd say now's as good a time as any." She winked, stood up, and held out her hand. It was time to see some of

Blue Collar Romeo

those images. Or better yet, make some of their own.

Blue Collar Romeo

coming April 11, 2017

About the Author

Jenny Gardiner is the author of #1 Kindle Bestseller *Slim to None* and the award-winning novel *Sleeping with Ward Cleaver*. Her latest works are the *It's Reigning Men* series, featuring *Something in the Heir, Heir Today Gone Tomorrow, Bad to the Throne; Love is in the Heir, Shame of Thrones; Throne for a Loop; It's Getting Hot in Heir; A Court Gesture;* and her new Royal Romeos series, featuring *Red-Hot Romeo; Black Sheep Romeo, Red Carpet Romeo,* and the upcoming *Blue Collar Romeo.* She also published the memoir *Winging It: A Memoir of Caring for a Vengeful Parrot Who's Determined to Kill Me,* now re-titled *Bite Me: a Parrot, a Family and a Whole Lot of Flesh Wounds;* the novels *Anywhere but Here; Where the Heart Is;* the essay collection *Naked Man on Main Street,* and *Accidentally on Purpose* and *Compromising Positions* (writing as Erin Delany); and is a contributor to the humorous dog anthology *I'm Not the Biggest Bitch in This Relationship.*

Her work has been found in Ladies Home Journal, the Washington Post, Marie-Claire.com, and on NPR's Day to Day. She was also a columnist for Charlottesville's Daily Progress for over a decade, and is the Volunteer Coordinator for the Virginia Film Festival.

She has worked as a professional photographer, an orthodontic assistant (learning quite readily that she was not cut out for a career in polyester), a waitress (probably her highest-paying job), a TV reporter, a pre-obituary writer, as well as a publicist to a United States Senator (where she first learned to write fiction). She's photographed Prince Charles (and her assistant husband got him to chuckle!), Elizabeth Taylor, and the president of Uganda. She and her family and menagerie of pets now live a less exotic life in Virginia.

Visit Jenny at her website at www.jennygardiner.net where you can sign up for her newsletter, visit her blog, or find her on Facebook and Twitter. And every blue moon she'll post adorable pictures of her pets on Instagram as @thejennygardiner.